MW00424694

The Topography of Hidden Stories

Julia MacDonnell

Fomite
Burlington, VT

ISBN-13: 978-1-953236-06-7
Library of Congress Control Number: 2020949781
Fomite
58 Peru Street
Burlington, VT 05401

3/1/2021

The stories in this collection have been published — some under different titles and in slightly different forms — in the following magazines:

River of Grace, *American Literary Review*
Violets, *Minerva Rising*
So Much Water, *Literary Mama*
Marie and Her Sons, *Ruminate,* (Nominated for Pushcart Prize)
Dancing with NED, *Alaska Quarterly Review*
Witness, *Many Mountains Moving*
Whistle Stop, *HAPPY*
The Topography of Hidden Stories, *Paper Street*
Nativity, *North Dakota Quarterly*
Red Stain on Yellow Dress, *Mangrove*
    Also performed as part of the Philadelphia's **Interact Theatre**
    Writing Aloud series
Weapons of War, *Briar Cliff Review*
Diana's Dresses, *Larcom Review*
Soy Paco, *Heart Quarterly* (Nominated for a Pushcart Prize)

For Dennis

Contents

RIVER OF GRACE

Ma was going to find the river — that's what she told me as the two of us drove north through the Adirondack Mountains in Daddy's Pontiac. This was no ordinary trip. As little as I knew, I knew that much. We'd left in the middle of the night, and my mother hadn't planned on taking me along.

The road, as far as I could see it, was full of steep upward turns and lined with frozen evergreens. Here and there, the tree line broke and the shoulder of the road fell away into valleys of ice that shined like steel bowls as we sped past. I didn't know the name of the road. I couldn't see any signs.

"The river, honey, I'm going to find the river," Ma said again. "That's all I'm doing."

I knew I was with her by mistake. I didn't even dare to ask where we were headed until we'd been on the road forever. By then the sky looked like an opal, icy blue and white but with deep cracks of red and orange, like something behind it might be burning.

Opals are my birthstone. They're mined mostly in Australia, and they are the most fragile of the semi-precious gems. Ma told me that once as we looked at a display of them in a jewelry store window — rings, earrings, bracelets and pendants, all set in gold, some paved with tiny diamonds — jewelry so beautiful I pressed my face against the glass to see better.

'Don't count on ever owning anything like that,' Ma said, tapping the plate glass with her fingernail, then pulling me away. 'Anyway, it's nothing but a mineral,' she said as we walked on. 'One that shatters much too easily to make them worth the price.'

The day my mother went looking for the river and I went with her by mistake, she was smoking, Lucky Strikes. She kept the white pack on the seat between us, lighting one after another from the lighter in the dashboard. She pressed it in and it popped out when it was red hot. She took it by the knob to light her cigarette. I'd never seen that thing before, didn't even know it was there, a cigarette lighter, right in front of me, all the other times I'd been in Daddy's car. As Ma smoked, I kept thinking *L.S.M.F.T., Lucky Strike means fine tobacco. L.S.M.F.T.* An ad on TV. When I closed my eyes, the letters danced behind my eyelids and the smoke burned my throat. With my eyes closed, it felt like we were driving in the wrong direction.

The only other place I'd seen my mother smoke was at my Aunt Sissy's when my father wasn't there. My father hated smoking. Drinking, too. Also, thumb sucking, nose picking, nail biting, knuckle cracking, hair twirling and other habits too numerous to mention. Daddy prided himself on his self-discipline, and he was raising us to do the same. That's what he said, more times than I can count.

Usually, when we were visiting Aunt Sissy's, Ma and my aunt drank gin and orange juice out of glasses that had once contained grape jelly, the best glasses Sissy owned, Ma told me. They kept the gin in the refrigerator with the juice and we kids pretended not to know. 'Baby, don't tell Daddy, please,' Ma said once after I sneaked a sip and coughed. 'Don't you dare tell Daddy.' Then she and Sissy laughed and laughed.

'Baby, don't tell Daddy, please,' Ma whispered earlier that night when I found her outside, pushing Daddy's Pontiac down our driveway. I'd woken up, and seen her from the upstairs window. I'd never been a good sleeper, something she often reminded about. I rushed downstairs and out to the driveway. When she saw me, she twitched and slumped over the hood like she'd been shot. She wore a clingy flowered dress and high heels. The white shoes and white flowers on her dress glowed in the moonlight. Collapsed over the hood like that, she looked the way she sometimes made me feel, all hope and power gone.

"You scared the shit out of me, you little brat," she hissed after a moment, panting a little, but still not standing up. I'd never heard her curse before, not even at Aunt Sissy's. *I took the wind out of your sails, didn't I?* I thought, repeating what she said to me when she was taking away something I wanted, or not letting me have something I did. *I took the wind out of your sails, didn't I, little girl?* My mother did not like me with wind in my sails. Now, by accident, I'd taken the wind out of hers, and right away I knew that I did not like her without it. Ma wasn't Ma without wind in her sails. We looked at one another in the dark, the space between us deeper than a river, but neither of us sailing.

"Well, don't just stand there, baby! Give me a hand," she said. She whispered but it was the same gay laughing voice she used at

Aunt Sissy's. "Four hands are better than two any time of day." I hadn't heard that voice for ages, not since we'd moved out of our house in Massachusetts, the house on the Fore River. I joined Ma by the chrome grill of the Pontiac and helped her push. The silver Indian watched us, and I wondered what he thought. Together we heaved against the car and finally it glided, silent and majestic, like a sloop on water, down our blacktop driveway.

"Now go grab some clothes and pee," said Ma, once the car was in the street. "Don't worry, baby," she whispered when I hesitated, "I'm not going to leave without you. I promise."

I rushed into the house and peed, not quite believing her. I put on the pants and shirt that lay rumpled on the floor beside my bed. Daddy snored in my parents' bedroom. The last thing I wanted was to wake him. The last thing I wanted was for him to see us. He'd blow a gasket. He'd do whatever he could to stop us. I couldn't think beyond that. My other sisters, even the twins, were sleeping. The house was warm and airless. After I rushed downstairs and out the door, the family it contained seemed like a dream, like something I was waking up from.

The Pontiac hummed at the corner, its taillights glowing. We were gliding through the dreamy darkness when Ma lit her first cigarette. I watched her, wondering if I knew who she was. Maybe that's what made me think again about Aunt Sissy's, and how, when we lived in our house on the Fore River, we always used to visit her. Uncle Nate was already gone. He'd left Sissy with the kids in a messy apartment over a gas station, a place that stunk of fumes, and the traffic never stopped zooming by out front.

My mother and my aunt would sit at Sissy's kitchen table, and smoke and drink and look through magazines, Vogue and Glamour, while painting each other's fingernails and putting makeup on each other. They also put lipstick and rouge on my older sisters and cousins but they said I was still too young. Usually Frank Sinatra sang in the background —*When skies are cloudy and gray, they're only gray for a day. So wrap your troubles in dreams and dream your troubles away.*

The last time we went to Sissy's, my mother told my aunt, and my aunt agreed, that I wasn't as pretty as my older sisters, Bethy and Kate.

"She'll never be as pretty, but she's a good sport," Ma said. "And she's got a nice smile, don't you think?"

I stood forever in the pinkish light of Aunt Sissy's gaze, wondering what a good sport was, but knowing that I didn't want to be one. I wanted to be as pretty as my sisters. Then Sissy looked back into the magnifying mirror on the table and tweezed some stray hairs from her eyebrows. "Personality counts more than looks any day of the week," she declared, and the two of them laughed some more.

Sissy said I'd probably lose my baby fat in a few years. After all, there were no other fatties in our family. And when I lost my baby fat, well, who knew what might happen? "She just might turn into a swan," Sissy said, and they laughed again.

Aunt Sissy's husband, my Uncle Nate, hadn't left her for another woman, but to pursue his art. Aunt Sissy told this to everyone, even if they didn't ask. He left her and their four kids so he could go someplace to paint in peace. Paint in peace. My mother and my aunt liked to repeat this, making the p's sound like small explosions. *Paint in peace. Paint in peace.*

Before leaving, he painted landscapes on the walls by all his children's beds, scenes of mountains and lakes and forests and one of the oceans. Once when we visited, my girl cousins showed us where my boy cousin, Joey, who was 14, had decorated his mural with boogers. The mural showed a sunset behind some mountains and the mountains were streaked and bumpy with his greenish dried up boogers.

My uncle also left behind many paintings, almost none of which were framed or hung. They were stacked on the floor or left leaning against walls. Several rested against walls from the top of a couch or chair. There was a portrait of my aunt, only with one eye and a bugle sticking out of her ear, on the toilet tank behind jars of Pond's cold cream and bowl full of lipstick and mascara. My uncle's other paintings showed things like a naked lady's bottom with a vase of flowers on top and a fox bleeding in a trap, but with a face very much like Sissy's. Several showed headless women's chests with funny things—horses' tails or oysters — where the nipples should have been. One of the chests did have regular nipples but when you looked at them really closely, they turned into serpent's faces with their mouths open just a little.

My cousins paid no attentions whatsoever to these paintings which tugged on me like magnets. Every time we went to Sissy's I went back to them when nobody was watching me. I wanted to see every single brush stroke. And afterward, I thought about them for a long time.

"Crazy crap," Aunt Sissy called them. "And he had the nerve to tell me I could sell them when I needed money." She kicked the one of the naked bottom with the vase of flowers on top. "But not a bad ass, ya think?" she asked my mother.

In our black Pontiac, with my mother smoking Luckies and the smoke hazing around so my eyes stung and watered, I looked at the woods along the highway but kept seeing back to our last day at my aunt's. As she drove, Ma's cheeks were flushed, and her eyes bright, the way they were at Sissy's. And I felt scared, the way I felt that day, knowing I'd never be able to guess what was coming next.

After finishing their manicures and make-up, my mother and Aunt Sissy made us tuna salad sandwiches. They told us they were sending us, me and my sisters and my cousins, all seven of us, on an adventure. Joey was going to take us to his clubhouse near the quarry. And maybe, if we were really, really good, Joey would take us to the quarry itself. He smirked when Sissy said this, then went downstairs to wait for us at the gas station with its bright red pumps and the attendants who ignored us.

While Frank Sinatra sang — *it was just one of those nights, just one of those fabulous flights, a trip to the moon on gossamer wings* — and Ma and Sissy sang along with him, swaying to the music, they mixed the tuna salad, spread it on white bread, wrapped the sandwiches in waxed paper, and put bread and butter pickles in the folds.

"In our day we were considered beauties, too, you know," Sissy told my sisters and my cousins, who hovered by the table, snitching pickles and potato chips. "You didn't get your looks from no place."

"No, the apple doesn't fall far from the tree," said Ma, and again they laughed and laughed.

I knew what Sissy meant about my sisters and cousins. All were slender blondes and redheads with long, shiny ponytails. But I didn't know what Sissy meant about 'in our day' — as if her day and my mother's day were past. Sissy was a redhead, my mother a brunette. Both were prettier than any movie star. They had green eyes and lots of wavy hair they wrapped in pin curls every night. That day, they rubbed their wrists with perfume from a round blue bottle. It had a picture of the Eifel Tower on it. The mixed smells of the perfume, cigarettes and tuna salad, along with Frank Sinatra singing — *Take my lips, I want to lose them; Take my arms, I'll never use them* — took up all the air. I couldn't catch my breath.

"Do you remember when we were pregnant, you with Annie and me with Elizabeth, and we were walking along Evans Street?" Ma asked Sissy, whose real name was Edith, which she hated.

"Do I ever! Why a car full of good-looking young fellas started honking when they were still half a mile away."

"Of course, they were approaching us from behind," Ma said, giggling some more. "We still looked good from behind. From that angle, we still had our shapes."

"But we had bellies out to here!" Aunt Sissy leaned back in her chair and stretched out her arms as far as they would go. "Why I could hardly walk."

"The car, a red convertible, pulled up next to us." Ma smiled like she was looking at the boys in the car, not at the sandwich she was wrapping in waxed paper, folding the ends just so. "Those boys were young, so young."

"Well, how old were we? Not more than 18 or 19 ourselves. Neither of us was over 20."

"But we were mothers. We already had children."

"Remember the looks on their faces when they saw our bellies?"

"They couldn't get out of there fast enough."

"But one of them said to me, Ginny, remember one of them said to me, 'I'd like to see you again, baby, when you drop that load. Remember?'

Ginny was Ma's nickname which I almost never heard. Daddy called her Mother or Virginia. Hearing her called Ginny turned her into someone else, someone I wasn't sure I knew.

Ginny and Sissy packed us sandwiches and potato chips and Oreos and chocolate milk in glass jars because Sissy broke the thermos. She was carrying it to the table, swaying and spinning to Sinatra — *I've gotta crush on you, sweetie pie. All the day and nighttime hear me sigh* —when the thermos slipped out of her hands. The glass lining exploded out, shattering into a million pieces on the floor.

"I'll be goddamned," said Sissy, leaning over the shiny silver pieces.

"Bad luck, like a broken mirror," said Ginny, but when I leaned down close, I couldn't see anything in the broken pieces.

They put our picnic into two grocery bags, then sent us on our way, down the back stairs.

"Don't get lost," they called after us, laughing some more.

When we were going down the stairs we passed the Fuller Brush men coming up. The Fuller Brush men had to go back down because the staircase was so narrow. Then Sissy came flying down behind us, saying in a loud voice, that she had to place an order. "An important order," she repeated, and one of the Fuller Brush men, holding a small brown suitcase, grinned at her and winked.

Outside, not far from a sign that said, No Smoking, Joey smoked a cigarette, which he crushed out with his heel when he saw us. Then we set out into the woods behind the gas station, along a path littered with beer bottles, old tires, a broken toilet bowl and rusted pieces of a truck. Once, a garter snake slid across our path and Joey grabbed it and shook it in our faces. My sisters and cousins screamed and ran.

"You don't scare me," I lied to Joey and the snake.

"It's the serpent, the sinful serpent," Joey yelled, then he threw it hard and it fell into the trees like a piece of rope.

We kept walking until we couldn't hear the traffic sounds anymore. Joey's clubhouse was in a clearing just before the quarry and beyond the quarry was the Fore River and across the river was our home, a lovely home, much nicer than Sissy's smelly apartment. When we finally reached the clearing, we'd walked so far I worried that we'd never find our way back. The trees were very tall and the light was shaded green. High above us, in one tree, was a wooden platform, planks of wood nailed and roped together, with a ragged green tent on top. Joey's clubhouse.

"You can't go up there until we eat and you've been initiated," he said to me. My sisters and cousins giggled. I didn't know what he was talking about, initiation, a word I didn't understand, one you might hear at church. At one edge of the clearing, a shelf of granite jutted from the ground. We sat against the granite ledge to eat our picnic. The bread had turned green and soggy from the pickles. I wasn't very hungry.

"What kind of the club is it, anyway?" I asked.

"The P.T.A.," he answered. "Ever hear of it?" The others giggled.

"Sure," I told him, because I had. I knew I'd heard of the P.T.A.

Joey nodded, chewing on his lower lip. "D'you want to be in the P.T.A.?" he asked. "Wanna join?"

The others laughed again, but as if from far away. Joey had bright blue eyes and yellow hair that fell across his forehead. The way he asked his questions made my mouth go dry and something tickle in my belly.

"Sure," I told his shining eyes. "Course I want to join the P.T.A."

I was the youngest of the cousins. My sisters often stayed at Sissy's and came home whispering about their adventures with Joey, their adventures in the woods, but I'd never been allowed to go with them because I was too young. It drove me crazy sometimes, because I wanted to so bad.

"D'ya know what P.T.A. stands for?" Joey asked, the others giggled.

"Purple titty," Bethie whispered. "Purple titty." Then she shrieked and laughed and bent over, laughing so hard I was afraid she might be choking.

"Purple Titty Association," said Annie, with a strange accent, French or maybe Spanish. She didn't smile.

"D'ya know what a titty is?" Joey asked and again I nodded. He reached out and pinched one of mine through my shirt. It hurt. "That's a titty," Joey said.

"When you grow up, milk squirts out of them," said one of the girls.

"When they get big, men like to look at them and suck on them," another said.

Then my sisters and cousins pulled me by my arms up onto the big gray rock. "Sit down. So you can be initiated. Into the P.T.A."

Their voices blended. I couldn't tell who was saying what. My heart pounded so hard, my chest twitched. But I kept seeing myself as one of them, with a long, shiny ponytail and no more baby fat. I could see the perfect me sharing their fun, their secrets. My sisters and cousins tugged my T-shirt, trying to pull it up over my head.

"No," I shouted. No, no, no, no, no. All their arms surrounded me. They were laughing, paying no attention at all to my *no, no, no, no.*

The cold sky outside the Pontiac throbbed, and the woods along the road shined with melting ice. It was daylight. I looked at the sky and then the trees, blurred with our passing speed, and wondered about this old memory, or dream, whatever it was, me trapped inside it, like I was trapped now in the Pontiac, speeding forward, moving, moving, moving and it didn't matter one bit how scared I was. It was going to keep on going, my mother with her foot on the pedal, her hands around the steering wheel, her eyes on the black snake of road ahead.

That day the girls, my sisters and cousins, kept pulling on my T-shirt, slapping my face, shrieking yes, yes, yes against my no no nos. No, yes. No, yes, slapping hard enough to hurt, slapping even harder than my mother did.

You have to, you have to, it's your initiation.

Their voices came from all directions.

You have to. Then you'll be like us. You'll be one of us.

Then through the shouting and the tugging and pulling and pinching I saw myself without the baby fat and with the long, shiny ponytail. At last I was alone up there on the big rock with just the greenish light around me. The rock was so hot, it burned my legs and bottom, but the rest of me was frozen.

"Go ahead now, pinch your titties," yelled Joey from the ground below. My sisters and girl cousins stood behind him watching. That's when I figured out that they were only kidding. They were making fun of me. I was a big joke to them. That's when I started making faces, and sticking out my tongue and waving my arms. They didn't laugh. My sisters held my T-shirt. My chest was bare. I stood up and jumped around on the rock. I waved my arms, still making funny face. I refused to pinch my titties.

"I'm warning you," Joey called.

I wanted to jump off the rock and run but the ground was way too far away.

"If you jump," said Joey, like he read my thoughts, "the sinful serpent's gonna get you. Now pinch your titties." The girls stood behind him nodding yes.

Next thing, I was squeezing those bits of skin between my fingers. It was embarrassing, like they were watching me poop or pee. I stopped. I shouted, "I don't want to join your stinky club. I hate your stinky club. It's stupid." Then I jumped, maybe thinking I could fly, fly away from them. Instead, the world went black.

I don't know why I woke up the night my mother left to find the river, except that I'm a restless sleeper and sometimes have to pee in the middle of the night. To get to the bathroom, I had to pass through many other rooms in which my sisters and the twins, the babies, slept. There were seven of us now, all girls, and everybody said Daddy would keep trying until he got a boy, a son to carry on the family name. One or the other of the twins was almost always whimpering. Sometimes it was like the sound of the doves outside our kitchen window. Other times, it was the sound I imagined a wounded animal would make. Sometimes, I'd hear these low cries when I was sleeping and my dreams would spin around them. I'd see myself crying in the dream, but for what, I didn't know.

Once, not too long before she left to find the river, I passed through the twins' room to the bathroom, and it was my mother who was crying. She sat in the rocking chair, rocking back and forth and back and forth, holding one of the twins wrapped in a blanket, and she was making an awful noise, the noise of a trapped and wounded animal. It made me think of my uncle's crazy painting. Ma didn't even see me passing through. She didn't seem to see me now, though I was sitting right beside her. She gripped the

13

wheel, a Lucky smoldering between the first two fingers of her right hand, and kept on driving higher.

Sooner or later, I got back to the apartment, running, running the whole way, the others chasing me, and shouting. I fell down a few times and Joey fell on top of me and shoved his hand between my legs so hard it hurt.

When we got back to Sissy's, Sinatra was no longer singing, and the Fuller Brush men were gone. Ginny and Sissy jumped up at the sight of me. The two of them looked blurry, their rouge and lipstick streaked, their hair wild, like they'd just survived a storm.

My sisters and cousins had rushed up the stairs behind me, all of them shouting at once, trying to tell their story before I could tell mine. I was jumping crazy on the rock, they said, jumping and running and pretending I could fly, and then I slipped and fell.

"We were with Joey, playing in the clubhouse when she fell," said Annie.

"That's when some bullies, teen-agers with sharp sticks, came along and hurt her," my sister Bethie added. "They cut her cheek and tore her shirt."

"It could have been much worse if Joey hadn't rushed down from the clubhouse and chased them all away."

Joey was no longer with us. It was just us girls. I suppose he was downstairs smoking. Their story didn't match my memory, but I liked theirs better. In mine, it was Joey who cut me with the stick. He did it the first time I tried to run away from him and he caught me and pushed me down. He cut me with the stick and banged my head against the ground and pinched my titties and warned me not to tell.

"I'll slit your throat if you do." His blue eyes were hard and see-through. "You know I could."

Blood trickled from my cheek into my mouth. When Joey was finished, my sisters and girl cousins pulled me up and put on my T-shirt. They hugged me and told me everything was OK because now I was one of them, a member of the P.T.A. Now I could play with them whenever I wanted and they wouldn't make fun of me anymore, even if I didn't lose my baby fat. Again I took off running.

Ginny and Sissy listened to the story, nodding and humming, and warm with sympathy. They brought me into the bathroom with the picture of my one-eyed aunt, and they washed me up and combed my hair.

"I didn't think you were old enough to be trusted with the others," Ma said. When I started to cry, she smacked my face. "Be quiet, or I'll give you something to cry about. You have some nerve, playing crazy like that in the woods. You could've been killed. Lucky for you, Joey was there."

She and Sissy washed me, and changed my T -shirt, giving me a clean one of my cousin's. Neither noticed the bruises, like fruit stains, all around my titties. Once I was washed and combed, Ma combed her own hair and reapplied her makeup. She piled us into the car and we headed home. On the way, she stopped at the Dairy Queen near the shipyard, not far from where we lived. She bought us ice cream cones, regulars for my sisters, but a chocolate dip, a double, for me. We ate them at a picnic table there because Ma didn't want us spilling in the car.

"Now, don't go telling Daddy," she told us, smiling, as she wiped traces of ice cream from our mouths and fingers. "Let this be our little secret." Not one of us ever again mentioned that day at Aunt Sissy's. And soon we moved away.

I don't know why I woke up or looked out the upstairs window. I don't know why, when I saw Ma heaving herself against the Pontiac, my heart stopped. But I went downstairs and out the back door. It seemed to be part of a dream. Ma looked so small in her clingy summer dress and high heel sandals. Still, the Pontiac slid back a couple of inches every time she heaved. I could see the down slope of the driveway and knew that at some point, gravity would take over, and pull the big sedan out into the street. I imagined that, once the car got moving, Ma would leap onto the hood, and the Pontiac would bear her off, soundlessly, into the night. And later, when I thought about my mother at her river, I imagined her gliding upon it, queenly, in this quiet, gleaming vessel.

Ma brought nothing with her but her purse, which at first I didn't realize. What concerned me was the weather. Why, I asked her, why don't you wait until summer, because the river might be frozen now?

She didn't answer for a long time, and when she did, she said it wouldn't matter, the river being frozen. I couldn't argue because I didn't know much about rivers and nothing at all about her plans. Not far from where we were living then, were the Susquehanna and the Hudson, mighty rivers both, with many tributaries. But I hoped Ma was talking about the Fore River, the one by which I'd been born, and near where Aunt Sissy and my grandparents and all my other aunts and uncles lived. We used to be able to see the river from our bedroom windows and across it, smoky and distant as a moated castle, was the shipyard where most of the men and women in my family worked.

But we moved not long after that day at Aunt Sissy's and several times since then. Like an angry Bedouin, Daddy moved us through coastal towns in Massachusetts, New Hampshire, Maine. After that, he turned west, first to the mountains of Vermont, then to the mountains of upstate New York. We didn't live in tents, or carry our belongings with us. We rented houses filled with other people's furniture. Time and again, Ma warned us not to harm the beds or chairs or couches or make marks on the walls. She said she wanted to leave the houses just as we had found them, looking like we'd never been there.

In the Pontiac, I finally asked Ma, "Is it the Fore River? Are we going back?" I thought we could move back into our old house, and start over, just Ma and me. That our old house would be there by the water, clean and empty, ready for the two of us. I'd finally have my mother to myself, and maybe then she'd love me. This idea beckoned through the windshield, vast and dazzling as the opal sky.

"Oh, no, no, no," she said, turning to look at me. "No, honey, we're not going back to the Fore River. We're not going home."

"What river then? What river are you looking for?"

"The River of Grace," she answered. "The River of Grace is where I'm bound." She looked so happy when she said this, I couldn't ask her any other questions. I'd never heard of the River of Grace and it worried me, but I couldn't seem to tell her. Of course, at home, we said grace before every meal. And at church, the priests were always talking about grace, a state of holiness you could achieve by being very, very good. But I doubted Ma's river had to do with anything like this. I also felt certain we were going in the wrong direction, up, instead of down. I wondered if we might be looking for the river's source, but I couldn't ask this either.

We kept on driving higher. Once we heard Sinatra on the radio, his voice so clear he might have been there, with us in the car. *How far would I travel to be where you are? How far is the journey from here to a star?* I heard Ma's harsh intake of breath, turned to see her hunched over the wheel, her eyes closed, like there was something on the road she couldn't bear to see. *And if I ever lost you, how much would I cry?* She pulled herself together just before we slid into a ditch. The car picked up speed, and Sinatra went on singing. *How deep is the ocean? How high is the sky?* My mother held the radio's glass face until Sinatra's song was over, and then she shut it off. Afterward, in the silence, I kept thinking about the River of Grace. I wondered if it was anything like the Fore River. I wondered if sunlight shined on it like handfuls of tossed sequins. I wondered if schools of minnows flashed in it shallows, and if oil slicks swirled colors on its surface — magenta, gold, green. I wondered if children played upon its muddy banks, or swam there in the summer. But I never asked.

I didn't get to find the river with my mother. She left me off before she found it, turning off the steepening highway at a sign for a city whose name I'd never heard before. By then the sky was icy blue but without the pink and orange cracks. The fire behind it had gone out. We drove around the streets, where snow and ice were melting in the sun, and the streets and sidewalks glistened. We passed a school with yellow buses lined up out front. I figured Ma didn't know where she was going, that we were lost, but finally we passed through a downtown with banks and stores, and ended up at a building with a billboard of a Greyhound bus on top. We parked and went inside.

Ma pointed to a scarred wooden bench. "Wait for me," she said. In a while she returned with a coconut cruller and a paper cup of hot chocolate. "Your favorite, honey," she said. "Eat. You'll feel better."

Then she pressed some coins and bills into my hand. Coconut was Bethie's favorite, not mine. I preferred cream filled. When I finished eating the donut, and drinking the hot chocolate, which wasn't hot at all, she took my hand and walked me to a bus with a driver already sitting behind the wheel. The motor was running. The bus seemed to be trembling.

"The driver knows where you're getting out," she said. "He'll tell you. Then go to a pay phone. You know what number to call." She smiled and patted my cheek and walked me up the steps onto the bus. "Sit here, right up front," she said in a loud voice so the other passengers could see and hear what a good mother she was. "That way you get to see everything. You'll have the best view."

She leaned down close and I smelled the perfume from the round blue bottle. I expected her to warn me not to tell Daddy. Instead, she hugged me and took off, flying down the bus steps and out the door. Ma didn't wave to me. She didn't turn around. I watched her rushing through the terminal, a pretty woman in high heel sandals and a clingy summer dress, though it was not yet spring. Just before she disappeared, I thought nobody would have ever guessed where she was going, searching for the river.

Whistle-Stop

THE MCHUGHS, ALL EIGHT OF THEM, piled into the family's brand new Plymouth station wagon — finned, chromed and white-walled — bought off the lot just a few days before. They were happy, so happy, the McHughs, and also proud of their ark even though they knew, every one of them, that pride was a sin, a deadly sin.

A pilgrimage!! They were going on a pilgrimage! That's what Jack McHugh was calling it, and Annie, the third of his six daughters, knew from catechism that a pilgrimage was a holy journey. A holy journey. This phrase had circled in Annie's mind since the night before when Daddy announced his plans at supper. *A holy journey.*

When they piled in, Annie grabbed her new favorite spot, in the 'way back,' a rear-facing seat where she could hide from her sisters and was beyond the reach of her parents' swinging arms and flapping hands, the sudden face smack or head crack being Jack and Leona's favored method of control, and Annie, her opinion anyway, being one of their favorite targets.

Daddy backed out of the driveway and turned right into the street. Annie watched their tract house, a 'For Sale' sign out front, shrink into the distance like a dream slipping away.

"We're headed into history, girls," Daddy declared, then gunned the motor so the station wagon shot forward like a rocket. "Today's gonna be a day for the memory books!"

Annie sighed and hugged her knees. She knew what her father would say next; knew it well enough to mumble his words to herself. *JFK would be president someday! Yes, John Fitzgerald Kennedy would become the first Catholic president —Irish Catholic, no less! And a Democrat, too, a Boston Democrat like the McHughs!*

For days, Daddy had been repeating this same spiel: If JFK — so young, so dynamic — didn't make it in November, well, he surely would in '64! What a great day that would be!! A great day for Democrats and Catholics, but also, and above all, a great day for Irish Catholic Democrats from Boston! A great day for the McHughs!

"You girls, why you'll be able to say you've seen the president!" Mom chimed in, turning toward her daughters. "The president of the United States of America! How many other kids you know can say that?"

Not one of the six daughters — they ranged in age from one to 15 answered. Maybe they were awed. Maybe they were bored. Their pink-cheeked freckled faces gave nothing away.

"A little bit of history being made," Daddy intoned as the silver station wagon sped toward its destination: an airstrip on the bay side of Long Island where JFK himself was scheduled to appear. "Can't wait to shake his hand, to tell him he's got my vote!"

The station wagon zoomed out along the flat roads, past miles

of developments — grids of straight streets crammed with identical houses —past shopping strips shoved up against highways;
past gas stations, burger stands, car dealerships, drive-in theaters
— sprawling and glistening in the cool October light.

"You know, girls, no Catholic has ever been president," said
Dad, segueing into his oft-repeated lesson about New York gov-
ernor Alfred E. Smith and how his Roman Catholicism had been
used against him in his 1928 presidential campaign against Herbert
Hoover. "Blatant bigotry," Dad finished, emphasizing his alliteration.
"That's all it was. I was just a boy, a young boy at that time, but I saw
latent bigotry turn into blatant bigotry during that ugly campaign."

Annie stretched her legs out across her seat, luxuriating in her
distance from the others, precious space she rarely found in their
overcrowded little house, one they'd soon be moving out of, and
Annie, for one, couldn't wait. Here, in this comfy spot, Daddy's
disembodied voice became an atmospheric hum. Her entire life,
all twelve years of it, Daddy had been lecturing them, her mother
and her sisters, telling all of them what to think, what to believe;
allowing no challenges, no interruptions. Sometimes she seemed
to hear him even when she was asleep. Before she herself could say
the word, Annie knew she was a Democrat. She knew that being
a Democrat was like a state of grace, a privilege you were born
into. Democrats, after all, believed in racial equality, social justice,
internationalism, and in the basic goodness of the common man.

"My, sweetheart, how things have changed!" Dad cried, punch-
ing the horn once as a bicyclist wobbled from their path.

Sometimes Annie's father embarrassed her and angered her,
but his excitement over Kennedy was contagious — an affliction
that caused moments of crazy optimism, spasms of joy. Today,

from this seat where she could not see where they were going, but only where they'd been, Annie watched the passing landscape — streaked and flattened by their passing speed, already disappearing by the time it came into view. She felt lucky, yes, lucky as could be. Why, she was on her way to see the man who would be president one day! She, Annie McHugh, the third of seven daughters, every one of whom her parents hoped would be a boy, was about to see a future president. How many other kids could say the same?

The station wagon — the color of a jet, Daddy said the day they bought it — was a nine-seater and they filled it to capacity: Jack, tall and handsome, behind the wheel with his petite and pretty wife Leona beside him. Two or three of their little girls were climbing over her lap while the two oldest — Amy and Beth —sat in the middle seat whispering about their boyfriends, Elvis Presley and their hair. Annie thought their conversations were stupid and boring. She wasn't mature enough to understand, they told her

"A whistle-stop by plane," Daddy said as he guided the station wagon onto the expressway. "Proof positive we're living in the modern age!"

Annie couldn't see her father, but she imagined him, leaning forward, hugging the steering wheel, the awesome power steering, his fedora pushed back on his head. Like his own father before him, Jack McHugh always wore a hat, a good hat, felt, with a band of dark grosgrain, maybe a small feather. One remarkable thing about Kennedy, Jack McHugh pointed out, was that he never wore a hat. No hat! He had that head of thick Irish hair and all the money in the world, but he never wore a hat! Took guts, self-confidence, in Jack's opinion, to go out into the world with nothing on your head.

"You know whistle-stops won the election for Truman in '48,"

Daddy continued, his voice tight and twanging like that of the salesman who'd sold them the station wagon. Annie half listened, drowsing in the motor's hum, the swaying of the ark.

"He squeaked past Dewey by stopping in every puddle jump town there was. Whistle-stops all through the South, the Midwest, the Northeast. Back then, the campaigns traveled by train. Back then, not so long ago, really, they figured that was hot stuff. Trains. Hah! Truman would stand on the platform at the end of the railroad car. With the train stopped at the station. He'd stand for hours talking to people, shaking their hands. And it worked, goddammit, excuse my French, because he won, didn't he? Now Joe Kennedy, that old thief, why, he's gone and bought his son an airplane!"

Annie heard her father's laughter and saw him in her mind's eye, trembling with mirth, other feelings she didn't understand.

"A Convair passenger plane," Mom interjected. "Which Jack named for his daughter Caroline. Imagine! Girls, can you imagine?"

Silence.

"He's mobbed everywhere he goes," said Dad. "Record breaking crowds. People cannot stay away! So you girls have to stick together. And stay by us. I don't want anybody getting lost. No catastrophes, please."

"No catastrophes," Mom echoed. "No lost children."

Annie turned in time to see her parents glance at one another. Just that summer, her baby sister Ava had wandered off their blanket at Jones Beach. It was a sweltering July day and the search for Ava had seemed endless — throbbing sky, pounding waves, and a quiet sea of sunning humans indifferent to the McHughs's loss, their terror. Then, from an impossible distance, came the screeching of a lifeguard's whistle. Annie saw them first, blurred by the ocean mist, two lifeguards standing on their tower. One was blowing his whistle and the other was holding Ava up high in both arms. The lifeguard holding Ava turned round and round, a slow pirouette to show off his find. Ava, in a yellow bathing suit, kicked and flailed like she was trying to swim or run away. Afterward, at home, she got a royal beating, and was put to bed without her supper. She had to learn her lesson.

"You know what Jack Kennedy's got that nobody in this tired old world has had for ages?" Jack McHugh asked no one in particular. "He's got charisma. Which means a powerful personal magnetism." He spelled it slowly: C-H-A-R-I-S-M-A and repeated it, charisma, said it was from a Greek word meaning a gift or favor from the gods.

Annie, however, already understood about JFK's charisma even if she did not have a word for it. She understood in a place without words that Kennedy was a sorcerer who had made her parents' sorrows and confusions disappear. Since early summer, Jack and Leona had been swept up in Kennedy's campaign — "He'll get the country moving again!" — and talked of little else.

At noisy family dinners, above the squabbling of his daughters and Leona's incessant reprimands, Daddy explained what the Kennedy candidacy meant to people like the McHughs, the children and grandchildren of poor immigrants, exiled during The Hunger. That Kennedy's appeal, despite his wealth, was to blue-collar workers and to the disaffected. His campaign was about hope, about the future!

Kennedy's opponent — Tricky Dicky — was hardly worthy of consideration in Daddy's opinion. 'There are other names for him I can't use at the family table,' he'd say, then glance at his wife and wink. Nixon, after all, favored big business and the interests of the

wealthy! And the foreign policy of the Eisenhower/Nixon admin-
istration was a proven disaster!

During family suppers in their tract house with the 'For Sale'
sign out front — the McHughs were moving to a big house near
the water — Daddy told his girls how JFK's older brother Joseph
—Joe Jr. — had been killed on a bombing mission during World
War II and how his sister Kathleen had been killed in a plane crash
soon thereafter. How Joseph Sr. —who couldn't tell the difference
between right and wrong even when the Nazi threat was staring
him in the face — had made his fortune bootlegging whiskey but
then had turned around and bred his sons for public service! How
Joe Sr. figured he was buying respectability when he bought himself that ambassadorship to England!

'Still he's nothing but an old thief and an adulterer,' Dad
repeated and laughed as if Joe Kennedy's trespasses were a good
joke on everyone. 'That's why Jack has put a muzzle on him. That's
why Jack hides him in a closet!'

Jack McHugh's figurative speech was lost on Annie who pic-
tured the white-haired Kennedy patriarch imprisoned in a lightless
cubicle, not unlike a confessional. Which was only right and just,
Annie felt, considering.

Yet the sins of fathers should not be visited upon their sons,
Jack McHugh said often. JFK was his own man in spite of his
wealth and privilege. Why he'd been bred for public service! He
believed in labor unions and in the goodness of the common man!

"I'll put my few cents, my vote, on the son of a millionaire any
day," Daddy went on. "That's because a rich man has no motiva-
tion to be corrupt. No sirree! He already has more money than he
knows what to do with!"

"Yes, but he's a realist, honey, not an idealist," Leona added, reciting her lines enthusiastically. "He'll get things done! He'll get the country moving again!"

Drowsing in her parents' words, Annie re-examined, like a beloved heirloom, her family's Kennedy connections, the shared background that made her family what Daddy called "the genuine article, Kennedy's people." Not only did JFK and Daddy share the same heritage and given name, but they were just about the same age and had grown up just a few miles apart in Brookline, Massachusetts. During the McHughs's last visit to Boston, Daddy drove past his own childhood home, a dilapidated triple-decker, then past the Kennedys' sprawling white colonial. 'So near and yet so far away,' he murmured to his wife and Annie, eavesdropping, wondered what he meant.

Not only had these two Irish Jacks grown up at the same time, within walking distance of each other, both of them, veterans of World War II, had suffered back injuries during the war! Both underwent back surgery after coming home! Their injuries still tormented them from time to time and whenever this happened, both wore custom back braces! Lately, Daddy had taken to showing his off —a contoured leather contraption, like a polio corset or a flat saddle, with straps and buckles. He showed it off to neighbors, chance visitors, the mailman, the milkman. 'Jack's is identical, and believe me, it's murder,' Daddy would say and no one ever doubted him.

Daddy and JFK had even gone to the same university, Harvard, though at different times and by different routes, Daddy on the GI Bill, "not my old man's money. Exact same degree, though! Which is the beauty of America!"

Jack Kennedy had been elected to Congress from Massachusetts' 11th District where the McHughs had lived before moving to New York. 'I voted for him then and I'm voting for him again,' Daddy vowed at least a million times.

Once Annie, worried about her family's status as Kennedy's people, the genuine article, had asked her father how the McHughs could be Boston Democrats when they now lived in Bay Shore, New York. 'Oh, honey, you can take the family out of Beantown,' Daddy answered with a big grin. 'But you can't take Beantown out of the family!' The McHughs were still Bostonians —'dyed in the wool!' — and always would be even if Jack earned his living elsewhere.

It was that living, as a labor lawyer, that had uprooted the McHughs from their ancestral home, separated them from their big devout family, and set them down in this flat place, on the bay side of Long Island, where everyone talked funny and nobody they knew went to church.

Here, where the McHughs were as odd and marginal as refugees, Annie sat at the supper table listening to her father's loud voice, watching his strong hands flap around to emphasize his words, and she understood that for him a dream was on the verge of coming true. She didn't understand the dream, had no idea what it really meant, the Kennedy candidacy, or her parents' passion for it. All she knew was that it mattered, more than anything had before.

"You know, Kennedy shakes so many hands, his own end up swollen and bleeding." Daddy slowed near an off ramp, piloting the ark around a coiling cloverleaf. Again the big Plymouth picked up speed. "He'll be in terrible pain — a couple of small bones in his hands have been crushed — but he'll keep on going. Because he loves meeting the people. Thrives on it."

Annie saw Kennedy's hands, swollen, bleeding as if with stigmata, and inside his bruised skin, the small bones crushed. She promised herself that she wouldn't squeeze too hard when she finally got to shake his hand.

Then she imagined their destination: a jetport with glistening hangars and big jets gliding down smooth runways. She imagined seeing those big jets up close, imagined running her palms along the steel skin of the Caroline. She imagined Kennedy waiting there for them, the McHughs, his people.

Annie was floating in these daydreams when she remembered she was wearing her new coat, the one she'd gotten for her 12th birthday a few weeks before. A bright blue poplin car coat trimmed with white fake fur and red and black embroidery. It had a big ugly zipper up the front. Annie almost died when she'd pulled it out of the box. She'd been hoping for a navy blue wool car coat with toggle buttons. She'd believed with all her heart that that's what was in the box. She was so shocked she managed not to cry while her family sang Happy Birthday to her.

"I hate this ugly thing, you can't make me wear it," she told her mother a couple of days later when forced to put it on for school, seventh grade. Leona conceded that the color was "a little bit off, kind of bright," but she was adamant. "That's a top quality coat, a Weather Tamer, you ungrateful little brat. I bought it just for you at Dalrymple's. It's a gift I've given you with love, and I'll be darned if I'm going to bring it back." Annie realized then that her blue coat was a clearance item, a final sale, something nobody else had wanted.

'Blue, blue God loves you,' Beth and Amy taunted when their mother couldn't hear. 'Electric blue — He couldn't miss you.

Annie's fantasy jetport turned out to be a mud and gravel airstrip, flat and empty as a square of cardboard. Just beyond it glimmered Great South Bay. They turned off the highway and joined a long, slow procession of other pilgrims in sedans and station wagons. "I'll be jiggered," murmured Daddy as he pulled into the line. Annie saw more and more cars behind them, an infinite snake that slithered across a rutted field, over a tarmac runway, and into a makeshift parking lot. Cars were parking every which way, their antennas swaying in the brisk wind, their windshields shimmering with fans of light. All around them, parents and kids were slamming car doors, dashing out to the edges of the runway.

"Record-breaking crowds, I told you, Mom," Dad said. The McHughs scrambled out, too. "That must be where she'll be coming in." Daddy gestured to the sky above the landing strip. It was huge and empty but with a border of puffy clouds that made Annie think of the fur trim on her coat. The ground was sodden, puddled everywhere. Leona, after those awful moments at Jones Beach, tethered her four youngest together with a long pieces of red ribbon. She herself would hold the ribbons. As an added precaution, she pinned onto their jackets cardboard nametags shaped like flowers. After a long argument at home, Mommy and Dad agreed that the three oldest could be spared the pins and tethers as long as they promised they wouldn't let their parents out of sight.

"This is history, girls, history," Dad repeated as the family pushed its way through the throng. "I can't wait to shake his hand. Tell him he's got my vote."

The music of an ice cream truck bounced on the cold wind and bouquets of bright balloons, menageries of inflated monkeys, snakes and panthers, in pink, purple and orange, and American flags, hundreds of little flags, bobbed above the crowd, more people than Annie had ever seen together, even more than at Jones Beach.

As they made their way out to the runway, she was rankled by the swarming hordes, annoyed that these others had reached the runway before them. She thought that the McHughs, who were the real thing, after all, ought to be allowed to stand in front.

"Isn't there a special place for us, Daddy?" she finally asked.

"A special place?"

"You know, for us, the genuine article, Kennedy's people."

"These are Kennedy's people. That's why they're here, Annie."

"No, I mean for the special ones, like us, you know, the real thing."

Daddy laughed, a hard, bright sound.

"Hey, Leona," he called out to his wife, "Annie here thinks we McHughs deserve a reserved spot right out there in front. Cuz we're the real thing. What do you think?" He grinned from ear to ear.

"Oh, Annie," Leona cried, shaking her head. She tugged along the little girls who were attached to the ribbon leash like prisoners on a chain gang.

"There are no privileged characters in America," Daddy said to Annie, not smiling anymore. "Everyone's created equal. That's its greatness! That's what this campaign is all about!"

Annie understood the importance of equality, but she was still annoyed when the McHughs joined the masses at the runway. Those others couldn't possibly be the real thing, the genuine article. Even if they happened, by several strokes of good fortune, to be Irish Catholic Democrats, for sure they weren't from Boston, too.

But Annie soon lost herself in the crowd, its wild energy, an experience that felt similar to what happened during mass at the Consecration. When the priest said all Catholics, praying together, made up the Body of Christ. These eager and adoring multitudes were the body of JFK. And right away she realized that the body of JFK had its own wisdom: it understood the exact spot where the Caroline would emerge from the clouds. Annie watched the sky — it throbbed with clouds and hidden light — but sometimes she turned to look at her parents, whose faces were lifted to the sky, expectant, in a way she had not seen before. The two of them, Dad and Mommy, Jack and Leona, not her parents anymore, but instead only part of the one body, lost in the moment and the crowd even though they were visible, standing right there, close enough to touch.

"We know not the hour," said Dad after an age, "but he'll get here, he will." He told Leona to buy Good Humors for the girls, and Annie did not turn hers down though she knew it was childish, eating ice cream while waiting for the future president to appear. Mom, for once, was oblivious to melting ice cream and chocolate on her daughters' cheeks, fingers, and coats.

Not for another age, however, not until thousands of necks were cramped and eyeballs scorched from gazing at the sun, not until the body writhed and hope seemed to be in jeopardy, did the Caroline tumble through the clouds. She fell toward the runway like a ball of fire, of light. A roar went up. The voice of the one body, not the wind, seemed to buffet the plane.

The gleaming aircraft zoomed toward them, tilting to the left and right. The body of JFK screamed — the Caroline, with its precious cargo, looked so precarious, so fragile. Finally the Caroline touched down, and skidded, screeching, down the runway. The body surged back. Gasps and shrieks and cries. A fierce current pulled Annie this way and that, swept her into a throbbing darkness. She saw only a sliver of the scene: the Caroline bouncing over gravel, spewing up dust, clots of mud, stopping beyond reach.

When Annie regained her vision, the massive body bobbed between her and that radiant thing, the Caroline. And the McHughs, goddammit, excuse my French, the McHughs had been shunted to the far edges of the crowd! Not fair! thought Annie. When she turned toward her parents, she saw their faces still uplifted — they looked dumbstruck, maybe paralyzed.

Another roar turned Annie's head. That's when she saw him hovering above them: John Fitzgerald Kennedy, grandson of immigrants, son of an old thief and a philanderer, a presidential candidate! Sunlight rebounded off the airplane's silver skin and JFK stood smiling in the dazzle. He stood waving in the Caroline's open doorway, but seemed to float on air. A whistle-stop by plane!

JFK raised one hand and the voice of the one body hushed into reverential silence. "The real issue of this campaign isn't religion, not mine or anyone else's." His voice, his living vibrant voice, with its broad vowels, flattened R's and nasal tones crashed over Annie like a Jones Beach wave. Trembling in its wake, she heard only bits and pieces of what JFK said next, something about the real issues being hungry children, and elderly Americans who couldn't pay their doctor bills. Inadequate public schools, disgraceful city slums, an inept foreign policy.

"Because I'm a Catholic, the real issues are being obscured," said Kennedy. His words throbbed through Annie, an echo of something the McHughs already knew, already understood. "It's apparently necessary for me to state once again, not what kind of church I believe in — for that should be important only to me — but what kind of an America I believe in!

"Did I give up my right to run for president the day that I was baptized?" John Kennedy asked, the response so wild and potent the earth shifted under its weight. When it settled, Annie's heart galloping and neighing, JFK urged everyone to vote. *Be sure to register, and make sure that all your friends registered, too, because I need every single vote.*

"The truth is," Kennedy cried out, chopping at the air with his hands, the light shimmering around him, "my father told me he's not going to buy one more vote than is necessary. Joe said he'll be damned if he's going to pay for a landslide!"

The body quaked; mirth and joy surged through it. *That Kennedy! His father wouldn't buy one more vote than necessary! He'd be damned if he'd pay for a landslide!*

Annie didn't get the joke. She'd never heard of buying votes. She turned to her parents. They were holding one another, tears glistening on their cheeks, laughing in a way she'd never seen them laugh before — as if JFK and all he stood for, belonged to them, and them alone.

The one body was still quivering when JFK disappeared. Boom, like a magician, gone. The one body groaned and bellowed, but Annie realized he'd gone down the steel steps of the Caroline and stepped into the crowd. A whistle stop by plane! He was in the crowd, shaking hands! Annie saw her parents still embracing, reverence on their faces; her silly sisters huddled around them. Part of the one body, frozen on the spot. Annie checked the edges of the crowd, looking for a break in it, her chance to get closer. 'So near and yet so far away,' Annie thought as she thrust herself forward.

Afterward, Annie will not remember how, exactly, she made her way to him. Will not remember how many toes she stepped on or the cracks in the crowd she managed to squeeze through. Will not remember circling the crowd's perimeter, her saddle shoes sinking into the wet earth, the mud oozing up over the sides. Will not remember unzipping her horrible coat, slipping out of it, molting it, leaving it behind in the pressing mob, because she could not greet the future president in that awful coat. She will not remember the voices, the throbbing darkness, the smells of wet wool and perspiration.

She will remember being pulled toward him by some force larger than herself, larger than anything she'd ever felt in church, larger even than her parents. And she'll remember coming out into the light and seeing him right in front of her, John Fitzgerald Kennedy, the Irish Catholic Democrat who would be president some day. She'll remember how bright the light seemed to be and how her hand fluttered out and hovered in the vibrant air surrounding him. Yes, the air itself felt different there — unsettled, like the air near the place where lightning strikes! Or how she sometimes felt during mass, at the moment the priest turned the bread and wine into the body and blood of Christ.

JFK's hand enfolded hers, pressing like a promise as he searched the crowd for her face. Annie's eye, her proud green Irish Catholic eye, her Democratic eye, appeared cyclopic in the crack between two wooly shoulders. She'd jammed her face between them. There, her eye devoured JFK's white grin, his auburn hair, his hazel eyes, his cashmere Chesterfield. It devoured, too, the thing you couldn't see but only feel —the energy, the charisma.

"What's your name?" the candidate asked Annie's eye and he

leaned in close to hear her muffled whisper: "Anne Marie McHugh, the daughter of John and Leona, who used to live in Brookline."

She felt her hand enfolded. Forgot her promise not to squeeze too hard.

"Well, Anne Marie McHugh from my own hometown," he said, "you tell your mother and father to vote for me, O.K.?" Annie's heart slid down her arm and out through her hand into his. "Annie, you tell John and Leona that their votes are important to me, all right? Promise you'll make sure they get to the polls?

The rough wooly shoulder of a man beside her shifted, slamming Annie's skull. Her torso was vised tight by opposing segments of the famished body. "We're the real thing, we McHughs," she shouted into the darkness. "Boston Democrats...Irish Catholic, too..." A hot pain skittered up her arm to the place where her heart had been. JFK was gone.

Annie gasped for breath, buffeted like the Caroline, with loss and cold and a hunger that had nothing to do with food. But she also felt what might be jubilation: she was rising above the crowd, like her baby sister when the lifeguards found her, only nobody was holding her. Maybe like Jesus when he walked on water at the Sea of Galilee. *JFK said my name and shook my hand! He asked me to get John and Leona to the polls!*

But where were they? How would Annie find her family? These questions came to her along with an alarming realization of the one body's depth, its breadth; with her realization that she'd lost her coat, molted it, a terrible old skin. Perhaps she was lost. Or maybe she'd been found. She couldn't say for sure.

Annie walked, but could not feel her feet, or the ground beneath them. She walked and walked

"There you are, you brat!" Leona McHugh's voice, coming from a distance, pierced Annie's bubble. She plummeted back to earth. "Where have you been? You scared us half to death."

Far away, too far to reach, Annie saw her mother. She held the blue coat, the empty blue coat, covered now with mud, trampled, its white fur brown and matted, the little sisters, still tethered around her, silent. "Imagine how we felt when we found this!! We thought you'd been snatched."

Annie held out her anointed hand. She tried to find the words to tell them what had happened.

"You disobeyed." Daddy swooped toward her through a gaggle of bystanders. "You defied my orders."

Several of them turned to watch.

"You've ruined our day. Wrecked it. Once again," said Mom. When Annie was close enough, she shoved the coat back at her. "Put this on right now. You brat."

"Little Miss Independence," added Dad, a lamentation to the gathering crowd. "All I wanted was to shake his hand, to tell him he had my vote. I wanted to take part in a little bit of history being made. Instead I had to hunt for you."

"When I saw your coat in the mud," cried Leona, "I thought it was your body."

"So sad," shrieked Beth or Amy. "We thought you were dead."

Annie believed she could redeem herself if only she could tell them what had happened, how she'd shaken hands with him. She'd never wash her hand again. Again she held out her hand, waved it in front of him. Daddy slapped it back. His Harvard ring strafed her palm. A drop of blood seeped out. "Don't dare raise your hand to me, young lady."

Leona turned vaguely to the crowd. "More of her sneaky stuff. How many times have I said she's always up to something."

The conflict still bubbled when Annie heard, from the runway, the whine of a departing airplane. The rest of the McHughs, and all the others heard it, too, the plaint of the Caroline as she lifted off. They turned to look, silenced by her piercing cry. She plunged into low clouds and was gone.

Annie's eyes were still glued to the sky where the Caroline had been when Daddy smacked her. The blow, to the side of her head, knocked her back to her senses. The crowd began dispersing. Daddy shoved Annie once, twice, maybe three times, until her ankle twisted and she stumbled. She struggled to stay upright. The other McHugh girls —the four youngest still attached to Mom — scurried toward the station wagon. Annie, holding her muddy coat, limped the rest of the way. When they reached the car, Daddy unlocked the tailgate and Annie leaped inside before he could shove her again.

"Wait till we get home," he threatened, slamming shut tailgate.

She'd get a royal beating. For sure. And after that, her mother might not speak to her for days. She'd be made to launder the blue coat and to wear it even if the mud did not wash out.

"You ought to be ashamed of yourself," Mom called back to Annie. "You ruined our special day and you ruined your new coat. If you think I'll buy you another one, you better think again."

"All I wanted was to shake his hand, to tell him he has my vote." Dad turned on the ignition. "To take part in history being made."

The McHughs, in their silver ark, joined the procession back out across the muddy field, Daddy again hunched over the wheel. He hugged the awesome power steering, his fedora pushed back on his head. Silent now, the McHughs headed home to their tract house with the 'For Sale' sign out front. The gleaming ark picked up speed as it raced over flat gray highways, past miles of subdivisions and shopping strips.

Annie, shivering, tucked her muddy feet under the furred edge of her Weather Tamer and looked out at the sky where the Caroline had gone. Maybe her coat was ruined but she didn't care. At home she'd get a royal beating. She didn't care about that either.

"Troublemaker," Amy whispered

"Gonna get it when we get home." Beth.

The voices of her sisters chorused from the shadows behind Annie but she didn't listen. She couldn't see where they were going, only where they'd been. She saw this clearly even if she did not want to. Beneath the blue coat, she held one hand in the other. Her right hand throbbed, a grace or an affliction. She wasn't sure and she wondered if it mattered. She kept watching, all the way home.

THE TOPOGRAPHY OF HIDDEN STORIES

"CALLS HERSELF AN ARTIST," Daddy liked to complain behind Aunt Ceci's back, harrumphing, and sucking his tongue, as though Ceci, short for Cecelia, and pronounced Seesee, had just proclaimed herself the emperor of France, or maybe the Messiah. Daddy, who swelled and quivered anytime he had an audience, almost always said these things in front of my other aunts, his sisters, three pale silent women, who'd nod and sigh and press their palms together like Daddy had just spoken The Word, and that The Word had come to dwell among us, not merely from him, my overweight and overheated father, making faces in our kitchen, but from the Father of Us All, God himself in heaven, and that His Word was the light shining in the darkness.

What really got Daddy going was the summer when Auntie Ceci began designing a collage, a gigantic one, on a slab of fiberboard so big it took up the entire wall of the dining room where she worked.

"What in hell does she think she's going to do with the damned thing?" Daddy asked everybody except Ceci. "Doesn't she notice it's too BIG to hang on a wall? Can't she see it's too BIG to move out of the dining room?"

Daddy shouted the word 'big' whenever he asked these questions, flecks of spit exploding off his lips.

This happened back when we girls, my three sisters and I, were still at home, still growing up. Back then, Ceci lived right around the corner from us, in the family home my grandparents had left her, the only one of their many offspring who'd failed to marry, to have children. Daddy and my aunts — Ceci's own sisters — always said it that same way, that Aunt Ceci had failed, as though marriage and motherhood were tests she wasn't smart enough to pass. As for her creativity, what Daddy called her 'nutty so-called art,' he and the aunts theorized she did it because she didn't have enough real work to do. If she had children to tend to, meals to prepare, laundry to get done, they reasoned over steaming cups of freeze-dried Nescafe, she'd have no time for such nonsense. Then they'd whisper, faces lowered to the cups, that if Ceci had more responsibilities she would likely shirk them anyway.

Aunt Ceci was a skinny nervous woman with bright young eyes in a shriveled face. I figure she stopped buying new clothes somewhere around the 1950s. She wore scarves, tied at her throat, and capri pants and ballerina slippers from the first time they were stylish. She'd gloat when she saw them now on models in my sister Clara's *Seventeen* and *Mademoiselle*.

"Everything old is new again," she'd say, smiling and nodding to herself.

"Certifiable," said Daddy, twirling an index finger by his ear.

Ceci ignored Daddy, no matter how mean he was, but she

loved talking to my sisters and me. And I, for one, loved listening even though I didn't always understand her. At the beginning of her project, for example, she told us that 'collage' had become her "most congenial medium ... That's because it gathers together diverse fragments and makes of them a new unity, a wholeness."

Ceci, who warmed to an audience even faster than Daddy, always talked to us that way, as though we mattered, like we had brains, not Marshmallow Fluff, in our heads. Maybe that's why I loved listening even though I often had to look words up.

Before Auntie Ceci became a fulltime artist, she'd held many different jobs, proving, at least to me, that what Daddy said about her couldn't be true. Among the jobs I knew about were editorial cartoonist, commercial photographer and typesetter at the local newspaper, not exactly work for a whack job, a dim wit. She'd also, by her own account, explored several diverse streams of art — first training as an actress and a dancer, and then expressing her vision as a portrait painter, a singer/songwriter, a choreographer, a performance artist.

"See, she's always been a nut, a fruitcake," said Daddy when I tried to point this out to him.

As for her most recent endeavor, Daddy and my aunts agreed, rolling their eyes and clucking, that Ceci was better off as a collagist than as a performance artist, when she'd made a public spectacle of herself, singing off-key songs and dancing awkward hopping dances in hand-made costumes at church socials and various municipal events like the Memorial Day parade. My sisters and I listened and didn't disagree, even though we knew, or at least one of us did, that what they meant was they were better off. We never pointed out how exciting it had been that Easter when Auntie

Ceci interpreted, to a taped score by Aaron Copland, the agonies of the Virgin Mother after she witnessed the crucifixion of her only son.

The four of us were squeezed into three seats in the front row of the church basement where we tried to memorize her movements. After the performance, when some of the nuns were weeping, but Daddy was flushed the color of a pomegranate, and my other aunts had disappeared, Auntie Ceci gave us her costume, shimmering blue drapes, almost see through, for playing dress up. My sisters and I took turns using this costume, making our own leaping, spinning dances until Clara, the oldest, decided to keep it for herself, and never danced in it again.

Maybe Ceci was a nut, but my sisters and I loved her. All our lives, we'd been drawn to her as if she gave off magnetic rays or flames. It was something not one of us could explain. Some people, including the pastor of Our Lady Queen of Peace, told Daddy she must be our mother figure, filling in for the one we lost in a car crash when, Grace, the baby, was just two years old. But the ones who said that only proved they didn't have a clue about us girls, or about our aunt.

Every chance we got, we'd go over to her house, making up excuses about helping her with some small chore or other, bringing in the mail, or hanging laundry outside on the line. We'd stand at the back door singing out her name like carolers, "Auntie Ci, Auntie Ci." She'd answer the door as though she'd been waiting for us, swinging it open as wide as it would go, and laughing and calling us her peas in a pod, her litter of kittens. "I get the biggest kick out of you, you plural," she cried, enfolding us in her bony arms.

Which is how I happen to know that Auntie Ceci's work with

collage, and what she began to call "the big job," actually began with a cleaning binge in the basement of her house, one that eventually brought her up to the dark dusty third floor attic where she discovered crates and boxes of her parents' things. "A treasure trove," declared Ceci, insisting that my sisters and I follow her up into the dim space, laced everywhere with cobwebs. Breathless, we crouched beside her, looking at the birth and death certificates, old photographs, marriage licenses, Christening clothes, letters and postcards going back at least three generations.

"Ancient history," Daddy sniffed when we told him, as though Auntie's treasure trove were just old junk. He suggested filling a couple of oil drums in the back yard, squirting on the lighter fluid, dropping in the match. "Poof. That's it, done. What's the point of keeping it?"

Daddy didn't seem to expect an answer and he didn't get one. Daddy was, however, outvoted by his sisters, the usually silent ones, who decided that the contents of the boxes might, at some point, prove interesting to one of the many grandchildren. That they might, somehow, contain a meaning even if that meaning was not immediately clear. At the very least, they'd keep Aunt Ceci busy. So Ceci, with our help, lugged the boxes downstairs and even Daddy lent a hand, complaining all the while. She began going through them right away, intending, she announced, to organize and catalogue all that they contained.

"I'm inspired, energized," she kept saying after Daddy left and the four of us were flopped around her, sweaty and exhausted. The fading papers, photographs, contracts, letters, newspaper articles were giving her a new perspective, she said, the great panorama of our family's history in these United States — its immigration from the southern coast of Scotland to Nova Scotia, to the Pacific Northwest and finally to the South Shore of Boston where the shipbuilding industry promised, falsely it turned out, long and lucrative employment.

Aunt Ceci announced to us that day and afterward to anyone who'd listen her plan to develop a grand and detailed history of our family; one that would include not just its achievements, but also "its peccadilloes, its dark secrets."

"Good luck to her and her invisible friends," said Daddy when we told him. My sister Margaret, supposedly the smart one, insisted a peccadillo was a musical instrument until I looked it up.

As it turned out, however, surprising me and my sisters but not our father, Aunt Ceci had trouble making the words go together; trouble sitting still long enough to write a sentence, a paragraph, let alone the grand and detailed history she'd imagined. Then one day, agitated and frazzled, she hit upon the idea of collage. "That's it, yes, I'll utilize the tangible remains, the flotsam of our lives, the things themselves," she told us, as if divulging a great secret. "I'm a mover and a shaker, not a sitter and a thinker. That's why the collage makes perfect kinesthetic sense for me."

The four of us listened, nodding as though we understood.

After that, a couple of my boy cousins brought the panel home from the lumber yard and, following Ceci's instructions, and with considerable effort, set it against the wall of the dining room, site of countless family feasts during the long decades of my grandparents' marriage. To create a workspace with good light — the dining room has a bay window with southern exposure — Ceci had asked Daddy to remove the antique dining room suite, walnut with pecan inlays, and put it into storage in the attic, empty now with all the crates and boxes moved downstairs.

"No, nope, no can do, no way, no how," Daddy answered, shaking his head. "You gotta be kidding me. In my book, dining rooms are for dining."

"Well, not in mine," answered Ceci, smiling as sweetly as one of the martyred saints in my prayer book. You could almost see the halo glowing over her head. So Ceci did the work herself, dismantling the table and moving it and all eight chairs into a spare back bedroom because she couldn't make the attic stairs under such a weight. We helped her with the chairs but didn't tell our father. After that, Daddy kept complaining that this room could no longer be used dining, but Ceci argued that it didn't matter because she wasn't a cook and didn't eat much anyway. On top of which, she pointed out to me and my sisters, but not to Daddy, our family has dispersed, scattering up and down the Eastern seaboard and rarely, if ever, getting together for a meal. No longer any of those big holiday feasts for us.

The summer of the big job got me to thinking about another summer, before we lost our mother, a summer so long ago that we girls might not be expected to remember. That's the summer when Aunt Ceci escaped the family and traveled throughout Europe. I think, but do not know for sure, that she was working as a photojournalist. Gone for ages, she went to Greece, France, Portugal, Italy and Spain. She returned with darker skin, a new accent, profusions of earrings, necklaces and bracelets, religious icons, exotic dolls in native dress and a boyfriend whose skin was even darker than her own. But Ceci disappeared again right after that, for years this time. She was gone for the rest of my grandparents' lives, and she did not even show up for Mama's funeral, and no one was allowed to ever speak her name. As far as I know, no one ever did. And when, at last, she reappeared, without any warning to us girls though Daddy did not seem the least surprised, she had nothing, no dolls, no jewelry, no icons, no boyfriend. That's when she moved alone into the old house, a ghost or a shadow of the fun, exciting auntie we had known, and she stayed that way until she discovered art, first singing and dancing to Biblical stories, and then moving on to our own family's history.

Aunt Ceci let us in to watch her work as long as we promised not to talk or interrupt. She worked every morning, getting up earlier and earlier. After coffee, she assembled her materials in small heaps arranged in a semi-circle on the old olive green shag carpet: old family photographs, mostly posed formal portraits, and bits and pieces of other family memorabilia, like an announcement of the launching of the USS Salem, a heavy cruiser, which my forebears helped to build, and my grandparents' invitation to the Kennedy inaugural ball back in 1960. Within reach was a little jar of Elmer's, the white kind with the brush inside the cap. From time to time Daddy would stop by, his excuse being my grandparents' old black Pontiac, which he kept buffed to a high shine, and in excellent repair, in the detached garage beside the house, just in case "Miss Artsy Fartsy decides she wants to drive again."

Auntie Ci never let Daddy interrupt her, but she seemed to sense whenever he popped in. She didn't turn to look, but instead pointed toward the door, her index finger quivering at the end of a long thin arm. Beat it, said her sign language, and Daddy silently obeyed, craning his neck to get a glimpse of the collage.

Most of the time, we — my sisters and I — huddled together,

47

on the floor under the bay window. "You're bearing witness," Aunt Ceci said once and she promised to paint us in that pose when she was through with the Big Job. Bearing witness felt important, especially because Daddy was not allowed to. Every now and then one of my sisters, usually Clara, but sometimes even Margaret, got bored and went back home, but I never did. I could have stayed forever in that space with its good light, where generations of my family used to eat and argue, empty now except for the Big Job, auntie's art, her work in progress. Gracie, the baby, my shadow, always stayed with me.

Aunt Ceci told us she worked by intuition, and I could see it was true. She fingered through her little piles for material that felt right, and filled in with her own drawings if she couldn't find exactly what she was after. She sang while she worked, usually Sinatra songs — *I've got the world on a string; Try a little tenderness* — and now and then she talked to herself. Whenever this happened, Clara and Margaret gave each other the wink eye, stink eye, and later would tell Daddy how loony she was. I never did. To me, her concentration seemed to squeeze out those whispered words. I strained to hear, but could never quite make them out.

Sometimes Auntie layered stuff on top of stuff, canceling out whatever was underneath, but creating what she called a "nicely textured topography" on the surface of the panel, and the "energy of hidden stories" within the work itself. Aunt Ceci predicted she'd be working for months, maybe even years, before the Big Job would be finished. Once it was, once Ceci was satisfied with all the stuff she had glued onto the board, and what she'd drawn when she did not have the right item to paste, she said she would shellac the surface several times, covering it with a hard yellowish shine that, she believed, would protect the precious items on the board, preserving them, and also, at the same time, giving the collage a mellow, aged patina appropriate to its subject.

That summer, right around the time that work on the big job had reached a fever pitch, Clara got her license. By then, Ceci looked frizzled, her capri pants stained and rumpled, her hair skewering off in all directions. No matter how early I got there, she'd already be working, surrounded by her little piles of family stuff and her pots of glue. Daddy kept saying that the little men were putting on their white coats and warming up the wagon to come take her away, a joke Clara thought was hilarious, and whenever she laughed, Margaret would start up, too, hee-hawing like a donkey.

Then one afternoon Ceci asked Clara to drive her back to the shipyard on the Fore River, near Quincy Bay, just south of Boston, where Grandpop, Daddy and many of my aunts and uncles worked from before the first world war through the Korean. With great sweeping gestures, and sparks shooting from her pale blue eyes, Ceci said she had to orient herself, to get a sense of history, of how things had been. She'd hit a snag in the Big Job, because there were no remaining photographs, if there'd ever been any, of our ancestors laboring to build the great ships, the cruisers and destroyers that had plied the waters of the world. We girls had to come along, she said. We were, after all, her witnesses.

Needless to say, Daddy wanted to do the driving, but Ceci insisted this was a 'girls only' adventure, and that Clara was old enough, or they wouldn't have given her her license. That shut him up. So one sunny afternoon, after listening to Daddy's endless directions and warnings, we put Ceci's easel in the trunk of the old Pontiac, and all five of us got in, Margaret up front with Clara, and Ceci in back, in the middle, between Gracie and me. All the way there, Clara clutched the wheel like she was afraid the Pontiac might escape, and every chance she got, she preened into the rearview mirror, checking her lipstick, not knowing how ridiculous she looked. Ceci sat leaning forward, chewing on her lower lip, as though we were heading to a shrine.

Back before Daddy started selling used cars on a big lot in Quincy, he'd worked at the shipyard, but he never talked about it. I don't even know what he did there.

What's done is done, he'd say when anybody brought it up.

For as long as I could remember, the shipyard had been shuttered and abandoned, its enormous buildings rusted into silence. You could see it from the highway long before you reached it, distant and misted like a moated castle, the Boston skyline glistening in the background. One of its docks had been refurbished for a commuter ferry into Boston, decorated with a ticket booth and a red striped awning. And a destroyer named the Ithaca, the last one built at the yard, had been turned into a museum.

But most of it was just the big empty buildings surrounded by iron fences with chained and padlocked gates. Queen Clara drove very slowly and carefully around them, as far as we could, until Auntie commanded her to stop. Gracie and I got out with her, carrying her paper and her pencils, special charcoal ones with nubby points. Ceci herself carried the easel, and she hurried, as though she might be late. Up a walkway, near an old hulk of a building, four stories high, lined with thousands of windows, all of them broken. The broken windows glittered in the sunlight, so high above my head they made me dizzy. Once I turned around to see where Clara and Margaret were, and they were watching from the car. Clara gestured at me through the windshield, waving us onward. I figured they were going to sneak a cigarette.

Ceci stopped, pointing to a corner window, shattered, high above the water. "That's where your grandfather served as a naval architect, designing the great ships," she said. "He worked his way up, apprenticing as hull rat at 14, and making architect by 30. Talent and persistence got him where he had to go."

I had no memory of Grandpop working, but as she spoke, I thought I glimpsed him, seated at a drafting table in that room high above the water, making architectural drawings of a ship, maybe a destroyer.

"What about Daddy?" I asked. Aunt Ceci laughed.

"Well, he didn't have to start quite so low on the ladder. He had a leg up, you might say," and she lifted hers to demonstrate, and laughed again. "But believe me, your Daddy was just as talented, a draftsman, one of the best."

I tried to imagine him, younger and happier, making drawings at a table in one of those rooms above the water, but I couldn't get a clear picture, just blurred wisps of somebody like Daddy but not really.

"You should have seen this place before and during the war." Now Ceci stood before her easel, a fuschia scarf tied at her throat, its long ends fluttering in the breeze. She stretched her arms out like a ballerina. "It was noisy, teeming, a world unto itself. There were the riveters and welders, the hull rats, the bucker-uppers and the lofts men. And always, always, a ship under construction up on the ways, draped with scaffoldings, crews of workers dangling along the sides. And the launchings. Wow. My God. If only you could have seen those launchings." Ceci waved her arms as though for a big crowd instead of only Gracie and me. "The christening of the ship, the slamming of the champagne bottle against its hull, the loosening of the ways, the great vessel plunging down into the water, then the great upward splash."

I wished I could have seen what she was seeing instead of the dilapidated piers, the shadows of the empty buildings, the quiet water.

"Everyone shared a sense of purpose. Everyone felt they mattered in the world."

Then Ceci began to draw with that fierce look she sometimes got so Gracie and I left her and went back to the car.

When we were younger, my sisters and I sometimes called her Seesaw. I don't remember which one of us thought of it, only remember that it seemed the perfect name to us because our aunt was hardly ever in balance and instead was always moving up and down, up and down. We loved the up parts when she would take us shopping and buy us everything we asked for, lipstick, Barbies, lace edged training bras. We hated the down parts when she seemed actually to shrink and couldn't or wouldn't remember who we were.

Clara and Margaret were sucking on Lifesavers and trying to wave away the smoke when we got back to the car. They were laughing and calling her that again, Auntie Seesaw. I remembered how, when we were really little, we'd compete with each other in the playground near our house to have the fastest ride on its deadly wooden seesaw. We called it that, deadly, because it was so big and heavy and we were always getting hurt on it, though we couldn't stay away. We'd take turns, two of us balancing the long board so the other two could climb on. We'd take turns kicking off, slamming it, pumping up and down, up and down, screaming, until somebody fell off, twisted an ankle or had the wind knocked out of them. Daddy forbid us to ride it after Margaret went home bloodied and wailing, but we sneaked back whenever he wasn't around.

"Auntie· Seesaw really is a nut; isn't she?" asked Clara in the snotty tone she'd recently developed. She was still clutching the wheel, though the motor wasn't running.

"You were smoking."

"If you tell, I'll kill you. I mean it."

Again Margaret laughed her donkey laugh, pointing at Auntie Ceci in the distance. "I mean, jeez, look at her out there, a nut." Clara started laughing, too.

"Yup, a nut," Clara repeated.

Granted, Aunt Ceci looked a little odd standing before her easel in the empty shipyard, a bright speck, her pink scarf lifted by the breeze. But to me she seemed to own it and to own what she was doing, calling back her memories so they came out through her fingers into the drawing on the easel.

"She is not a nut," I said. "She's an artist."

"Nut."

"Not."

"Nut."

"Not."

"Nut."

"Not."

We could have kept this going, a familiar kind of chant that would build in volume, intensity, until one of us gave up or punched the other. That day, I would never have given up. I'd have fought forever to defend my aunt. But Margaret, who was studying Spanish, interrupted us.

"You know in Spanish her name means yes, yes. *Sí, sí.* Yes, yes. Auntie Yes-yes."

"Auntie Yes-yes," cried Clara, spluttering and guffawing, like it was the funniest thing she'd ever heard, Auntie Yes-yes. Then all of us began to call her that, Auntie Yes-yes, in different voices and accents, even me, even though I didn't want to. We squealed and boomed, competing to be loudest as we watched her from the car, standing before her easel, pausing now and then, posing there, head lifted to the sky, as though waiting to hear the voices that would tell her what to do. Auntie Yes-yes. Finally, I couldn't stand it anymore. I got out, and Gracie followed, but then my shadow left me. She ran ahead, calling to our aunt that we'd renamed her, that she'd just been christened like a ship, only without the champagne. And when we reached her, Gracie cried, laughing so hard she could hardly get the words out: "You're Auntie Yes-yes. It's for the Spanish word *sí.* Aunty Sí! Sí!"

Auntie was quiet for a moment. I was afraid she might be hurt or angry because we'd broken the rule about interrupting. Then she twitched like some inner current had just been switched on.

"Yes, yes! *Sí, sí!* Es mi!" she cried with a Spanish accent, stamping her feet and striking a pose like a flamenco dancer. She didn't even need the rose between her teeth. "That is just so beautiful, so apt." Aunt Ceci hollered as though she were on stage, her eyes watering in a way that made me glad Daddy wasn't there, her voice echoing off the buildings, the water.

Then she leaned toward us, reaching out her arms. Gracie and I went to her, and she gathered us in, so close her scarf tickled my cheek, and she told us that she often, in her dark hours, read reflections by the late and great Dag Hammarskjold who had once served as the secretary general of the United Nations. And she told us the most important thing Dag Hammarskjold ever wrote was this: " ... at some moment I did answer Yes to Someone— or Something— and from that hour I was certain that existence is meaningful, and that therefore, my life had a goal."

To which Aunt Ceci added, "Yes, yes. Si, si! I do say yes to that." Again she stamped her feet and posed, and we giggled and she giggled with us, her eyes the palest blue, with the thinnest fringe of blond eyelashes. Eyes so pale you couldn't tell if they were deep or shallow. Si, si. Yes, yes. I do say yes to that.

Just as Auntie had predicted, her work on the Big Job turned into a career, her spurts of wild energy followed by periods of lethargy that bordered on paralysis. And when I came home for Christmas vacation during my freshman year of college, Auntie and the Big Job were gone and somebody else was living in the house. Nobody had told me anything.

"Was it the little men in the white coats, Daddy?" I asked him, furious that he'd kept this monumental news a secret. "Did they come to take her away?"

Daddy shook his head no, and I saw for the first time that his eyes were just like Auntie's, a shimmering pale blue, with hardly any lashes. I thought I saw in them the tiniest speck of sadness.

"It was me, honey," he said, more quietly than I'd ever heard him. "I brought her to a place where she could have a good rest. They can give her the help she needs. I didn't want to tell you while you were away. I didn't want to interrupt your studies."

"You should've told me," I wailed. "You should've let me come home."

I tried to tell him how I should've been there; how I needed to bear witness and how she needed me to. He didn't listen. He said the people in the house were only renting, that he hadn't sold the house and never would. "It will there for her when she's ready to come back," he said, though no one could say when that might be.

After that, I'd sometimes walk by the house at night, and I'd see the new family at the table in the dining room, which was, once again, being used for its stated purpose. I couldn't bring myself to ask Daddy about the Big Job. I was afraid of what he'd say. Or what he wouldn't say.

By then I, too, could drive. Whenever I was home, I went to visit auntie at the hospital in Wrentham, and sometimes I'd bring Grace. If we visited right after a treatment, electric shock, she'd be there-but-not-there, in a trance, and would not know who we were. Other times, she greeted us as she had at her back door — with open arms and laughter, her litter of kittens down to only two, and not kittens anymore. Then she seemed to be her old vivacious self, always involved in something, teaching other patients how to paint and draw and dance. On those visits, we talked about the family, and sang Sinatra songs. *My Way* was her favorite, while Gracie and I did mean rendition of *One More for the Road*. Everybody loved her there.

Once, when we visited, she was dressed up like a clown in a rainbow fright wig and was trying to teach the others the art of clowning. "You have no idea how liberating this big nose is," she told us, surrounded by a dozen or so laughing loonies, and she squeezed the red rubber bulb on her face. "You can do just about anything behind it."

That day, maybe because of her disguise, I got up the nerve to ask her if she'd ever finished it, the Big Job.

"Oh, you mean my masterpiece? My *tour de force*? My *piece de resistance*? My *coup de grace*?" She spoke with a French accent and with each question, took a funny little bow so the red nose wobbled. I nodded. She shrugged.

"Something eluded me. I couldn't quite get to the heart of the matter. It drove me crazy." She laughed at this irony. "At least your father thought so. I had to let it go."

"Where is it?"

"He knows, your father. He promised me he'd keep it. Just in case I got inspired again. Just in case I figured out how to finish it. Just in case I come home." Then she squeezed the rubber nose again and all the loonies giggled.

It wasn't that hard to find, covered in a couple of flowered sheets, resting against the wall of the garage, next to the old black Pontiac. It was just as big as I'd remembered it. At first I was afraid to lift the sheets and look under, though I can't say why. Then one day I did and I stood for the longest time in the dusty light of the garage trying to absorb what my aunt had accomplished, the great panorama of our family's history in these United States, its immigration from the southern coast of Scotland to Nova Scotia, to the Pacific Northwest and finally to the South Shore of Boston. Included in her collage were all the ships the men had built, and all the babies the women had borne. Using the flotsam of our lives, the birth and death certificates, old photos, newspaper clippings, cocktail napkins, tickets, matchbooks, along with her own paintings and drawings, Aunt Ceci had fashioned a grand and detailed history of our family; the family that had cast her out, first shunning her, then turning her into a dark secret or a joke. And I saw that, though words had failed her, as had her family, too, she'd embraced on that pressed wood panel all she'd known and loved in her own life, and all of those who'd gone before whom she might have loved. To me it seemed not just complete, but perfect. She'd taken diverse fragments and made of them a unity, a wholeness, and when I rubbed my palm across it, it throbbed with the energy of hidden stories.

That's what I would tell her the next time I went to visit her. She'd really done it: she'd finished the Big Job. Then I noticed, in the bottom right hand corner, fixed in bright acrylics, the four of us, my sisters and me, Auntie's peas in a pod, her litter of kittens, and we were huddled together there, haloed in the light from the big window, bearing witness.

Ceci. Yes, yes. I do say yes to her.

Red Stain on Yellow Dress

"Tell me what you'll be wearing, hon," says the woman on the phone. "You know, so I can spot you right away."

Serena, huddled in a phone booth outside Woolworth's, shivers despite the August heat. Her fingers, clutching the black receiver, feel as though she's shoved them into snow. She has trouble remembering her clothes. When she does, she eliminates most of them right away, her long skirts and her bell bottoms, her floppy hats and beads and feathers.

"Hurry up, honey," the woman urges. "I can't wait all day."

"Yellow, a yellow dress," blurts Serena, then hears herself describing one she'd sewn not long before as part of her plan to go hunting for a job as a receptionist or secretary. An A-line knit with cap sleeves and a jewel neckline.

"Bring cash, six hundred dollars in small bills, tens and twenties," the woman instructs.

"Sure," whispers Serena. She has about $400 rolled up in a nylon stocking in her room at Maggie's Farm.

"Your first name?"

"Serena," she answers, offering not her real name, but one she's given to herself, one she likes much better than her own. Janine, or Janny, as her mother called her, a name that wouldn't do at all for the life she planned to have.

"Now, Serena, when you get there, you just sit and wait. I'll find you, OK?" says the woman. "You'll know me when you see me. Red hair and sunglasses."

On the day of Serena's journey, Maggie's Farm, a commune on a bend in the Connecticut River, is very quiet. The hippies and the Trotskyists have left for the Democratic National Convention in Chicago and the outside demonstrations, the Festival of Life. Alone for the first time in ages, feeling herself adrift in the unaccustomed silence, Serena sits on her bed, holding the yellow dress she herself has sewn. Through the small-paned window, stubbled corn fields stretch for acres out to the new interstate. Soon she'll board a Greyhound that will carry her south along it.

Sitting in the dusty light, naked and still damp from her bath, Serena picks at the puckered seams of her dress, thinking about her mother, a seamstress who specialized in clothing for family celebrations. This time of year, August, when the First Communion, wedding and graduation rush was over, and the demand for holiday finery hadn't yet begun, she sewed cocktail dresses for herself, spangled wonders with spaghetti straps and low-cut backs, planning to get her singing career back on track. Once Serena caught her, decked out in a shimmering lame number, lip-synching to Sinatra in front of the full-length mirror in her sewing room. *I've got the world on a string...*

Fingering the yellow knit's plain bodice, Serena recalls her mother's hand stitching intricate patterns of seed pearls, rhinestones, sequins on bodices and veils, her fingers dipping into the glistening cups of beads, her needles flashing. The first thing Serena herself had sewn was a pink cotton blouse with a Peter Pan collar. When she'd finished, she rushed off to show her mother, who examined the garment carefully, then tugged at the tiny stitches, tugged until the pieces of pink cotton came apart.

"Too weak to hold," she said, handing the ruined blouse back to Serena.

Often, in this big house by the river, Serena imagines she's back in her mother's sewing room, amid falling scraps of fabric, with Frank Sinatra singing on the hi-fi above the humming clatter of the sewing machine. *I've got a crush on you, sweetie pie. All the day and night time hear me sigh...*

Before putting on her dress, Serena takes out her money, the $400 saved from modeling for life classes at the university, the other $200 borrowed from friends she will forget to pay back. She divides the cash into two equal piles, rolls the piles, wraps them in rubber bands and puts the rolls into her bra, one under each breast. When she crosses her arms under her chest, she feels the swollen lumps of cash.

By the time Serena gets off the Greyhound, after riding through the night, she is in the state of dreamy numbness she equates with higher consciousness. She has reached her destination, the nation's capital, much too early, but it was the best connection she could make from western Massachusetts. Following the instructions of the woman on the phone, Serena walks the length of the terminal — from her arrival gate to a bench facing the newsstand with a small American flag by the cash register. Through the nearest doorway is a shoeshine stand, not yet opened, and next to it, a blue mailbox, just as the woman had explained. Serena, as instructed, takes a seat on the bench, and tries to focus on the woman who will come for her, a woman with red hair and sunglasses. Red hair and sunglasses. Red hair and sunglasses.

As she had during the journey from Maggie's Farm, Serena worries that the woman will fail to show up; that they will not connect; that she, Serena, will be left waiting in the bus station forever, her body swelling, her mind disintegrating, her life over. For days, in dreams, Serena has imagined this woman coming for her. Once the woman was her mother, young and vibrant, hardly older than she, Serena. Another time, it was she herself, Serena, who arrived, and the girl she rescued was a stranger, plump and pimply, alone on a terminal bench in the bus station of an unfamiliar city. Twice during the night, Serena had thrown up, gagging over the bus's stinking toilet. Waiting by the newsstand, Serena feels again the urge to puke, but is afraid to leave the bench, to go into the bathroom, in the case the woman comes. She whispers the Hail Mary, *Blessed art thou among women, blessed is the fruit of thy womb.* The nausea passes but a corrosive fluid bubbles in her throat.

Then the woman's there beside her, sitting, and whispering. Serena turns and looks, sees the red hair is a wig, stiff and shiny as a helmet. The sunglasses are cat's eyes, with rhinestones at the comers, so dark she can't even see the outline of the woman's eyes. Her lipstick is bright red, applied in neat strokes beyond the edges of her lips.

"Serena," she repeats.

Serena follows the redhead out of the terminal to a blue Valiant, parked at a meter several blocks away. The woman begins to drive around the city and Serena becomes bedazzled by its buildings, majestic columned edifices, the White House, Lincoln Memorial, Washington Monument. These great structures, which Serena is seeing for the first time, are glistening in the morning light, at once deeply familiar and unreal.

The woman drives and drives and Serena begins to think they're going in circles, passing the same monuments, the same intersections. They drive until Serena emerges from her state of dreamy numbness and wants to scream or jump out of the car. Then the buildings start to change, growing darker, smaller, and at last, when Serena is no longer ready, the redhead pulls over. In front of them is a go-go bar with a flashing pink neon sign shaped like a bra. Next to the Valiant on Serena's side, a flowered couch tilts between the sidewalk and the gutter. Dark stains streak its cushions. Serena, staring out the window, wonders if they've reached their destination; if the procedure is to be performed here, on the flowered couch, in front of the go-go bar with the flashing neon bra.

"Have the money?" asks the redhead. She lights up a Marlboro, pulled from a flip-top box. Serena nods yes, but has trouble reaching down the neckline of her dress to get it. Finally she manages by sliding low into the seat and undoing her back zipper. The woman ignores Serena's wriggling. "You get what you pay for," she says, rolling down her window, exhaling smoke through the crack.

"Warm," she says when Serena hands her the two neat rolls of cash. The woman removes the rubber bands and flattens the bills out in her lap. She counts them twice, then puts them into her purse.

"Don't be scared, hon," the redhead says. She puts the Valiant into gear. "He's a real doctor. He doesn't make mistakes."

Now the redhead leads Serena into the living room of a small apartment. Its blinds are drawn, but no lights have been turned on. Several other women sit in the twilight waiting. No one turns when Serena enters. A small fan rotates on a coffee table.

"How long will it take?" she asks the redhead, her voice insubstantial in the still air. The woman shrugs.

"It takes the time it takes. He'll be as careful with you as he is with all the others."

The woman disappears, but returns in a moment. She hands Serena a blue pill and a paper cup of water. Serena, overcoming another impulse to throw up, swallows the blue pill with tepid water. In a while, she re-enters her state of dreamy numbness, and a mist seems to surround her. The other women turn into shadows, and one by one they disappear. Serena keeps thinking she will hear something. Weeping. Maybe the gnashing of teeth. She listens carefully, lids lowered, ears straining. She hears nothing but the whir of the fan rotating on the table.

The procedure is performed in the kitchen, on a table that is draped with white. Soon Serena, too, is draped like a piece of furniture, her feet strapped to the tops of kitchen chairs placed backward at the table. Lying on the table, she can see, through the window over the sink, a scrap of blue sky and wisps of cloud. The doctor is bald and he wears bi-focals, a surgical mask, a short-sleeved seersucker shirt. He is huge, puffy, like a plastic creature someone has inflated. His hands are big and pink. Serena has trouble looking at him, trouble watching as the woman with the sunglasses helps him put on the surgical gloves.

"This will be a routine dilation and curettage, Serena," he says, his words muffled by the mask. "I'll be opening you up and cleaning you out."

He clears his throat, draws Serena's attention to his instruments—the duck-billed speculum and the curette, a sharp-edged silver scoop. They glitter in his palms. "It will only hurt for a minute," he says. "Then you can leave here and go on with your life."

The doctor puts the fingers of one hand into Serena, probes the unripe fruit of her womb. With his other, he presses her belly on the outside. He nods, making throaty noises. "You're farther gone than you said," he says. "All you damned girls lie. Why?" He does not seem to want an answer and Serena does not give him one. The woman in the sunglasses stands in the doorway watching.

Now the doctor disappears into the white-draped space between Serena's knees. The speculum is cold and it squeaks as he cranks it open. He gives Serena no anesthesia but she is numb there anyway. Pain gathers elsewhere, shivering in her hips and ribs, skittering through her arms and shoulders, encircling her throat.

Serena hears the clanking of the instruments and the low voice of the doctor telling her what he is doing, a voice she doesn't want to hear. She does not want to know what he is doing, but she cannot seem to tell him. She cannot speak. Then she sees her mother's sewing room, the furniture and floor draped with clean white sheets to protect the fragile fabrics she fashions into gowns. She sees her mother surrounded by lengths of these fabrics: satin, tulle, taffeta, shantung; her mother, a hard bright thing, a stone, in this rainbow of luscious color; her mother, so small, hunched behind the big machine that she seemed always to be hiding. Her mother, humming along with Sinatra instead of singing words. *The summer wind came blowing in from across the sea...*

With the doctor hidden in the tent between her legs, Serena remembers how she used to hide under the sewing table; how, if her mother were working on a wedding gown, a ball gown, she'd drape the fabric so it fell like water to the ground and Serena, under the table, would be sealed into a shadowy world of translucent fabric. As the doctor works, and pain tightens like a drawstring around Serena's throat, she recalls her mother's scrap bag, the sack into which she dropped leftover fabric, all the pieces that didn't fit but were too good to throw away. Velvets, cottons, brocades in many prints and colors. Serena, hiding in her tent under the table, would pick through this sack, looking for pretty bits and pieces, making patchworks on the floor.

Serena tries imagining a design of shimmering pastels, but the patchwork will not come together. Instead Serena sees her mother, sees her mother watching, hunched behind the big machine, yet watching, her busy fingers working, her eyes as beautiful and empty as the jewels she sewed on other women's gowns.

"It's over, you're done," the doctor announces, his masked face rising like a moon above the mountain of Serena's knees. She is drenched with perspiration. Her arms and legs quiver as though the doctor had severed some essential bit of wiring when he'd cleaned her out. She cannot catch her breath.

"It's nothing, see," the doctor says, suddenly standing very close, holding out a steel pan, tipping it toward her. "See, it's just a bunch of cells."

Serena looks away but not before she's glimpsed the puddled blood and clotted tissue shining in the silver pan. The woman in the sunglasses comes and takes it. A moment later, Serena hears a toilet flush.

Serena is still vibrating when the woman tells her to get up and put on her shoes. "You're fine, you'll be fine," the woman repeats as she drives Serena back to the bus station. The trip is shorter this time. They do not go in circles, but instead head straight toward the terminal. Serena sees the sleek dog painted on its brick side, body outstretched, face and limbs straining in its race. Serena is wondering where the dog is headed when the woman pulls up at the curb and tells her to get out.

"You're fine, you'll be fine," she says again. "You should stop bleeding in about a week."

Serena finds her way back into the terminal. She realizes she's starving, and still shaking with the strange palsy. She searches through her purse for change, finds enough for a candy bar. She buys a Milky Way, eats it in one swallow. Then she has to pee, a need that announces itself as painfully as her sudden hunger. She rushes into the ladies room. All the stalls are locked with coin boxes. She is standing there transfixed when a woman's voice turns her around.

"Girl, look there. You gotta blood stain on your skirt."

A matron in a blue uniform is pointing at the back of Serena's dress.

Serena twists, looking backward, reaching for her hemline. The matron takes hold of the skirt, tugs it forward, until Serena herself can read the Rorschach.

"You got something to change into? Or at least a pad? You got a pad, girl?"

Serena looks at her. The matron shakes her head, puts some

67

coins into a box over the sink and hands Serena two sanitary napkins.

"Go clean yourself up," she commands, using her key to open one of the stalls. Serena obeys, her legs and fingers twitching. Still she cannot speak.

When Serena finishes in the toilet, the matron tries to help her wash the stain out in the sink. Serena stands close to her, half-backward to the sink, watching pink water splash through the yellow knit into the white porcelain of the sink. The outline of the stain remains, red as Hester's letter.

"Got yourself into some mess, huh, girl?" the matron says, wringing out the skirt, rubbing it with paper towels.

"It's just my period," Serena lies.

"Uh-huh," the matron answers.

They look at one another in the mirror, but Serena sees herself somewhere far beyond them: in a room by the river, hidden in a silky tent, the fragile fabric billowing around her. Again, Serena wonders what her mother would have told her if she'd been inclined to speak. But she cannot imagine. Because her mother hadn't been inclined to speak, only to keep her fingers moving, her silver needles flashing, while she hummed along with Sinatra singing on the stereo.

During the night, on the way back, the Greyhound's ventilated air blows like a mistral around Serena, chilling her while she sleeps. It gusts against the windows, whistles up from vents around the floor, slips through the crevices between the seats. Serena dreams that she is lost in a coastal storm; that everything she cares about has blown away. She wakes up chattering and shuddering. She wonders what it was she'd cared about, but no clear images stayed with her from the dream.

The bus is almost empty and she is sitting near the front. A transistor radio is attached with duct tape to the dashboard. The driver is listening to the news. Hundreds of protesters arrested outside the convention in Chicago, then hauled off to jail.

"Want my jacket, doll?" the driver asks her. "I can't do anything about that air."

Serena doesn't answer him. She doesn't acknowledge that he has spoken to her. He pulls into the next rest stop and brings her his jacket anyway. She does not thank him, but he does not seem to mind. Once the bus is underway, she curls up inside the jacket, its lining cold and slippery as water. It smells of tobacco and sweat. Serena draws up her legs, pulling them under the jacket. She feels blood spurt onto the Kotex and hopes the pad will hold. The jacket's lining warms against her skin, and Serena pulls it closer.

The humming of the Greyhound lulls Serena, but she does not go back to sleep. Nor does she listen to the news of rioting at the Democratic National Convention. Instead, through the Greyhound's wide windshield, glistening with reflected light, she watches the red taillights of the vehicles in front of them; the headlights of those traveling in the opposite direction. The passing landscape is blackened, lightless, as if they're boring through a tunnel, hundreds of miles long.

Serena's going back to Maggie's Farm but not for long. Where, after that, she doesn't know, but it does not seem to matter. Because she knows now that it is over. Soon she will stop bleeding. She can go on with her life.

Soy Paco

LA PERIODISTA, THE GRINGA JOURNALIST, sees the orphans whenever she drives past the plaza, *el zocalo,* of this ancient colonial city. She sees them, grimy street children, racing over white stones, begging pesos from homebound *trabajadores* or from artisans hawking blankets, baskets, shawls. She sees them begging scraps from women selling tacos warmed on smoky braziers; swiping oranges or avocados from the carts of peddlers.

Here they call them *los abandonados,* the children no one wants, some of them not yet school age, four or five years old. They've been flung out by the gyre of catastrophe, these little ones: earthquake, civil war, trade agreements, global recession. Left to roam in feral packs the streets and alleys of this city; to scavenge the stone teeth of the plaza, fighting one another with rocks and sticks, for the right to treasures — rags, paper, tin cans, who knows what— caught there by the night wind.

They've become a social problem, an embarrassment to the government and to the ruling party, *los abandonados.* Soldiers have begun to hunt them down — for sport and/or for higher social purposes. The lucky ones are shot in the head. Others may be rounded up, raped, tortured, for practice in the endless war against subversives, or merely for the fun of it. *La periodista*, the *yanqui* journalist, hasn't yet had time to report this story.

She is a trained observer, a gatherer of facts. Among the facts she has already gathered is this: *los abandonados* wear cast off gringo clothing; discarded shorts, T-shirts, jeans and sneakers — *los tenis* — sent through international relief by the mothers of billboard children in *el Norte*, bright-eyed sparkling youngsters who proclaim their caste with the name brands of their clothes, Hilfiger, Nike, Guess, J.Crew, American Eagle. When she's been surrounded, these logos catch her eye, signaling with bright wattage through the squalor. Gap. Boss.

During her years' reporting she has, however, learned that facts may, at some point, reach a state of critical mass; collapse beneath their own weight. This happens fairly often when she comes here to the plaza. When she sees the bigger children plundering the stashes of the smaller ones, the ailing and the lame, ruling them through terror. When she sees them, like now, at dusk, huddling in the shadows of the peddlers' carts, sniffing glue from Baggies and from empty screw top jars that once contained Gerber's baby food. The glue, manufactured here by a big *yanqui* corporation, and hardly ever used for sticking things together, is cheaper and more readily available than other forms of nourishment.

Toluene, an aromatic solvent in the glue, acts as a sedative and a hypnotic, immunizing *los abandonados* against fear, hunger, cold. Pungent, and venomous, toluene coils through their brains, their central nervous systems, comforting as mother's milk; satisfying as a meal of rich and varied courses, soup, grilled beef, *arroz y frijoles*, tortillas, chiles, spicy salsa. When they've inhaled enough, the children fall asleep on the white stones of the plaza as if upon a bed of down and feathers. But they wake up ravenous, mad, volatile as ether, their dendrites shrieking like the mothers of the disappeared.

The journalist hasn't yet had time to report this story, either. She does, however, consider possible angles, ways to pitch the story to her editors. A photographic essay strikes her as the way to go — she's knows they'd get some killer images — but her editors would have to fly down a photographer, and she doubts they'd be willing to spend that much on the story.

This evening, she has parked her little Hyundai in the shadows at the end of the plaza in hopes that she can avoid *los abandonados*. She hopes to avoid *los abandonados* because sometimes they surround her, or surround her car, small ferocious humans whose gender is uncertain, whose ages she cannot guess, whose language she speaks poorly though she understands much more. When they do this, surround her or her car, she becomes a hostage to her own fear until she gives them money to make them go away.

Not long before this evening, when the children had ambushed her and were moving in on her with their sticks and sharp edged stones, and she insisted to herself that she was not afraid, no, she had nothing to be afraid of, one of them, the shoeshine boy, had come to rescue her. Yes, the one-legged shoeshine boy who always set up — with his stool and a carton of cloths and polishes — on the plaza's southwest corner. This boy, with his crutch and his anger — *Vete! Fuera de aqui!* — had run them off and saved her.

He was, of course, an orphan, too, another of *los abandonados*, but he'd distinguished himself in at least two important ways: by his enterprise, shining shoes, which kept him from begging and/ or stealing; and by his refusal, so far, to seek refuge in toluene.

Since that rescue, however, the shoeshine boy has become another kind of problem, one the journalist has trouble explaining to herself. For now, whenever she was near the plaza working on a story, and she was often near the plaza working on a story, the shoeshine boy finds her and pursues her. Calls after her and sometimes chases her, hopping on his good leg and his crutch: *Senorita Yanqui, mi patrona linda, mi benefactor.* He sang these words, the shoeshine boy, giving the r's a melodic trill. She knew he was playing her, yet, almost always, his songs stopped her, turned her around. She would walk back, sit on the three-legged wooden stool — it rocked ever so slightly — and let him shine her shoes, usually sensible oxfords but sometimes pumps with a modest two-inch heel. Tonight, for the first time, she is wearing sandals.

As the boy worked, snapping his cloths so fast it seemed to be a circus act, he told her bits and pieces of his history. That he'd lost his parents, his sister, his home and his left leg, during *el gran terremoto,* the great earthquake, several years before. That he believed he had some relatives in the mountains, but hadn't yet been able to go look for them. That he was saving his money to buy a new leg. *Una pierna nueva.*

The journalist realized, while listening, that the shoeshine boy believed that he could actually purchase a new flesh and blood leg, not an artificial limb, a prosthesis. She didn't think it was her place to correct him.

Once she'd asked him how old he was, but the boy shrugged. He didn't know and the journalist couldn't guess. Like the others, he was so emaciated, so dirty, and his teeth were so bad, shadows of caries between each and every one, that the standard indicators of chronological age were inoperable. He seemed ancient, but his voice had not yet changed.

One detail, a fact, the boy had never volunteered, and the journalist had not asked for, was his name. She didn't want to know his name because without a name, she figured he'd disappear from her memory the way unnamed data sometimes goes missing on a hard drive. Without a name, he'd be irretrievable.

The journalist, however, did not always succeed in her efforts not to think about him. Images of the boy, like flotsam on a stream, often floated up from her subconscious when she was driving to or from her hotel, or drifting into sleep at night. Then she couldn't help wondering how he survived; how he protected himself and his money from the others. What protection did he have? Almost always, she managed to shove these questions back downstream.

Tonight, the journalist scans the plaza carefully. She tries not to acknowledge her own relief when she does not see him. But, in fact, the boy has spotted her and begins loping toward her through the shadows. She has just locked her Hyundai, beep, with its remote, when the boy, in his rush stumbles and falls against her. He grasps her arm to steady himself but the journalist, believing she is being mugged, flails and shakes him off. Floundering in the black water of her fear, she clasps her purse and tape recorder.

Buenas noches, senorita!

She turns her head, finds herself looking down into the shoeshine boy's grinning mouth while the black water ebbs. Jesus Christ, she mutters.

Lo siento! Tengo verguenza! My apologies. I'm so ashamed, he says as he backs away from her. He shakes his head, embarrassed by his clumsiness. *Lo siento*, he repeats.

The journalist looks at his empty trouser leg, and then at the unlaced Nike on his right foot. She can't find any words. Nothing comes to her.

Soy yo. Su amigo, he persists. *El major muchacho en el zocalo.* The best boy on the plaza. He grins and taps his chest, as if his proclamation were official: It's me, your friend, the best boy...

She nods, fear curdling into irritation.

No necesito un brillo, the journalist tells him. She points to her sandals, the perfect excuse. She does not want to tell him that she's in a hurry and has grown tired of their ritual, the shining of her shoes, a thin excuse for her charity. *No necesito un brillo.*

The words sound like a guidebook phrase: I don't need a shine. But the boy nods enthusiastically, indicating that it's OK. It doesn't matter that she does not need a shine tonight. They can still be friends.

Soy Paco, he declares then, again thumping his chest. *Me llamo Paco.*

He offers these words like a gift, but when the journalist looks into his eyes, glistening ingots, she feels them demanding something. What she does not know. She does not want to know. She looks away.

Soy Paco, he repeats, words that jab her like the sticks of *los abandonados.* She doesn't understand why the boy is telling her this now, this detail she doesn't want, his name. She pretends she hasn't heard him.

No necessito un brillo esta noche.

The boy seems confused by her repetition of the guidebook phrase. The tropical dusk is still and balmy. He reeks of excrement.

No hay problema. No se preocupe, he tells her.

In the dimming light, avoiding contact with his eyes, seeing instead the ancient marble of the plaza, the journalist recalls a dream, a fragment of a dream, in which she'd been with him, this wretched child, the shoeshine boy. In the dream, he'd had his new leg, a strong and vital limb. The two of them were walking together, bound together, moving together toward some unknown destination. He seemed to be the child she'd never had, the carrier of her genetic code, her DNA.

But now she, the objective observer, steps out of the dream and takes another look at him, a good one. This time she reads the filth that splotches his hands and cheeks, that mats and spikes his black hair, as a sign of his caste — not unlike the Nike 'swoosh' — an emblem of perdition.

Hasta luego, she tells him, turning away, heading for her interview.

Soy Paco, he calls after her in a bright, teasing voice. *Pero no se como se llama. Como se llama, senorita?*

I don't know your name. What's your name?

When she stops and turns around, he is there within her arm's reach. She opens her purse, rummages for a handful of small bills. She grabs the boy's rough hand for an instant while she presses the money into it — enough to feed him well for a couple of weeks if he can hide it from the others.

Pero no quiere un brillo? You don't want a shine?

She shakes her head no, looking toward her destination, a magisterial colonial edifice, yes, edifice, not building, surrounded by a high, spiked wrought iron fence, patrolled by many soldiers, silhouetted now against the smoky sky.

No. No necesito un brillo.

He shoves the money back at her. *Como se llama? Di-me su nombre.*

His imperative, Tell me your name!, is harsher this time. She's astonished by his arrogance. Who does he think he is? She will give him what she wants to give him, not what he wants to have. She presses the money back into his hands, a wad of wrinkled bills that are red and blue and orange. The two of them struggle with the cash, shoving it back and forth, until the bills are fluttering around them.

Adios, entonces, the journalist repeats once the money is out of her hands for good. She is breathless, trembling, but she recognizes her advantages: height, weight, two good legs. She resists the urge to shove him, to knock him to the ground. Instead, she takes off, sprinting toward the government *edificio* and her interview with the bureaucrat.

Soy Paco, the boy calls after her. *Soy Paco, soy Paco, soy Paco,* he calls and calls. *Soy Paco* he calls until his howl fills the smoky sky. *Soy Paco. Pero no se su nombre.*

DIANA'S DRESSES

Took Mom to see Diana's dresses because I figured it might cheer her up. Got caught in traffic just north of Boston where the interstates twine and tangle like veins inside a wrist.

"Guess money can't buy everything," Mom says, lighting a True Blue from the lighter in the dashboard. "So young, so rich, and those two young boys to raise." She frowns, exhaling a great plume of smoke. "Who'd a thunk it?"

"Crack your window," I say.

"Hmmmph," she answers, but presses a button and the window slides down half an inch. "Makes you wonder, doesn't it?"

"She wasn't wearing a seat belt, Mom. She was the mother of young children, no matter how rich she was, and she didn't buckle up."

"Her heart was ripped loose in her chest," Mom says, and I feel her withering glance, one she has perfected during the forty-something years of our relationship. "A seat belt wouldn't have saved her."

Now she is fumbling with the ashtray, which is stuffed with gas and toll receipts, the gate card for my parking lot at work, a spare ten-dollar bill I keep hidden for emergencies.

"Where do you want me to put this stuff?" I point to the glove compartment in front of her. "If she'd been wearing a seat belt, her heart probably wouldn't have been ripped loose."

She ignores me.

When Mom opens the glove compartment, my cell phone falls to the floor. Bending to retrieve it, she groans in mock agony. Then, squeezing her cigarette butt between her lips, she uses both hands to shove my stuff inside.

"Why don't you throw some of this junk away?"

Her question is a tiny laceration, a signal that we've begun yet another round in our endless argument about what matters and what doesn't.

"I always keep my receipts. Track my mileage costs. Make sure the gas and credit card companies aren't cheating me."

She makes a throaty sound, exhales in my direction. I'm furious about her smoking, but bite my tongue.

"My only vice," she declares, snapping shut the glove compartment, giving me the creeps with her ability to see inside my skull.

Again I bite my tongue, this time with greater effort. I could, and long to, list a few more: skipping breakfast, refusing to take dietary supplements, even calcium for her brittle bones, missing her P.T. appointments, drinking too much sherry, reading supermarket tabloids, watching trash TV.

"They say Dodi had just given her a half million dollar ring. A sapphire, I think. And it was lost in the wreckage."

"Wasn't it a diamond?" I ask, remembering something from '20/20.' "Worth about a hundred grand?"

"Whatever. I wouldn't turn it down."

Traffic inches forward and I put on my blinker, easing right toward our exit ramp.

Diana's dresses are on tour, a show called 'Dresses for Humanity,' which I think is grandiose, but my mother, a Diana nut long before the princess died, believes is a fitting tribute.

"You could look just like her," she's said to me a million times—as if I even wanted to. "All you'd have to do is style and highlight your hair."

"Lose thirty pounds and grow six inches," I'd reply, humiliated by her delusions, hoping nobody was around to hear.

The exhibit has been moving from one city to another, and I'd been tracking it, hoping it would stop somewhere where I could drive her. We do better getting out, not visiting at her place or mine. My house is misery because Mom doesn't like my kids, at least not as much as I think she should. She doesn't want to play Parcheesi with them or listen to them practicing their instruments — violin, piano, clarinet. "Been there, done that," she tells me. And I've come to despise the small apartment — up a flight of stairs and at the end of a dim corridor — where she's lived since Dad divorced her. It's hazardous and too expensive, but she won't listen. "It's my home," she says. "You can't afford it," I answer, which is all too true. Her Social Security check doesn't begin to meet her basic expenses. She's forced monthly to dip into the paltry sum she agreed to in her settlement. I figure she'll be broke in less than three years. "MYOB," she tells me every time I try to bring this up.

Diana's dresses are being exhibited in a museum created to honor America's textile history. I think I'm lost a couple of times before I find it in the middle of some huge old brick buildings, former mills, in the heart of Lowell. I pull up in front, let Mom out

and go to park. She waits for me on a bench outside, is grinding
out another cigarette when I return.

"You know I could've made it from the parking lot to here," she
calls out as I sprint toward her.

"Yeah, you could have, Mom, but the museum closes at three."
It's about eleven a.m. now.

"You're picking on a sick old lady," she tells me without rancor.
And I long to answer, but will not, that her ailments, except for her
arthritis, are mostly her own fault.

I pay cash, twenty bucks apiece, for us to go inside.

"But it's for a good cause, right?" Mom asks. "Land mines. Kids
with AIDS. Diana's charities."

I nod. The truth is, I can't believe I'm here; that I'm actually
shelling out hard-earned cash to look at a dead princess's clothes. I
won't tell any of my friends.

"I hope the John Travolta's here," Mom says as we join a line of several dozen others, mostly women. "I'm dying to see the John Travolta."

Mom means the long velvet number Diana wore when she
danced with the movie star at a White House dinner. She owns a
Diana doll dressed in a replica of that gown.

"It's not a John Travolta. Some designer, Victor something,
made it."

"Yes, Edelstein, in navy blue silk velvet. It's a beauty."

"Well, it's here. I already told you."

Since her stroke, a small one, Mom has used a cane to help her
keep her balance. She's refused to use a walker and vows she never
will. If she gets that bad, she tells me and my sisters, "Call Kervorkian." Once, in the rehab center, when she was crazed with pain
and anger, furious that her left leg wouldn't work the way it used

to, she made me promise I would. It was a pinkie swear. We linked baby fingers, and I vowed to call Kervorkian, a.k.a. Dr. Death, the minute she needed help to poop or pee; the minute she couldn't get around on her own. I promised she could count on me. She cheered up after that.

The cane is metal, with four rubber-tipped prongs on the bottom. Sometimes I think the prongs are roots, what's holding her on earth. Mom holds the cane in her right hand, so I stand on her left. Whenever I'm this close to her, I can hear her exhalations. COPD. Chronic Obstructive Pulmonary Disease. Several times a month she needs oxygen. The tank is set up in her living room where she can rest, watch TV.

There are benches in this waiting area, but my mother will not sit on them. Now that we're in public, she'll act as if she owns the world, her future. Which is doubtful. Our last outing, last week, was to North Shore Radiologic where my mother had an MRI scan of her brain.

Because the scanner, a stainless steel cylinder, was uncomfortable and the procedure a long one, they let me stay with her, told her to choose music from a rack of CDs. She chose Sinatra, *Songs for Swingin' Lovers,* but even Ol' Blue Eyes' seductive voice — "*She's never hungry for dinner at eight; she loves the theater but always comes late*" — failed to soothe her. Mom was shaking so much when they tried to slide her into that contraption, they had to stop and give her a Xanax, then wait for it to kick in. Even afterward, Sinatra's singing — "I've got a crush on you, sweetie pie" — couldn't conceal the clanging and groaning of the machine as it penetrated Mom's skull, making computerized images of her brain. I sat in a folding chair at the end of the table, holding her feet in my hands.

"Don't let go for anything," she called to me just before her torso disappeared. I didn't. I sat holding Mom's feet the whole time, murmuring, though she probably couldn't hear me, that it was almost over, she could do it, sure she could. Sinatra sang, the scanner clanged, and Mom quivered softly, terrified.

"I'd rather die than go through that again," she said when it was over.

Later, while Mom was getting dressed, the doctor offered me a guided tour of her brain. It was there before us on a screen, multiple views in swirling greens and blues and yellows, her right and left cerebral hemispheres, cerebellum, brain stem, sensory cortex, and motor cortex. Mom's mind, a distant universe. I felt like a high-tech peeping Tom as he pointed out dark places among the colors. Areas of atrophy, he said. Irreparable damage, done by a series of transient ischemic attacks, small strokes. Not just the one we knew about, but others, perhaps occurring in a cluster. Mom's brain, he said, resembled that of an eighty-five-year old, though she was not yet seventy.

"Why are you telling me?" I asked, feeling as if I'd just been rabbit punched.

"Because you need to know," he said. "Somebody must know. If she doesn't change her lifestyle ... well, let's just say, we could be waiting for the big one."

"The big one?"

"Major stroke."

Her lifestyle, that's rich, I wanted to scream. Instead I endured a violent bout of *agita*. Her lifestyle. Sitting home, smoking True Blues, drinking Bartels & James from a juice glass, watching Montel and Jerry Springer.

"You shouldn't light another cigarette," the doctor told my mother when at last she reappeared. "With a single cigarette you risk triggering a, a…a… " He seemed to struggle for the proper word. Major stroke, I was about to prompt when he waffled. "A cardiovascular event. A major cardiovascular event."

"Who, me?" Mom answered. She looked him right in the eye and gave him a dazzling smile. "I don't smoke."

When our turn finally comes to enter the gallery, Mom gasps, but not from her COPD. The room's so dark we can't tell where the walls are. Facing us is a larger than life-sized royal portrait of Diana. Just beyond it is a huge picture of her in a red suit hugging a sick African baby, and beyond that, looming out of the darkness, like obelisks on lunar plain, are the glass cases that contain, draped upon headless mannequins, Diana's splendid frocks and gowns. Light cascades from hidden fixtures above each one, glistening on silks, velvets, satins and brocades; shimmering on metallic threads and beads and sequins.

It takes a moment to orient ourselves. Then we focus on the first, a long burgundy velvet dress with a matching tailcoat embroidered with gold thread and pearls. A sign warns us not to touch the glass. Another says the dress was worn to the premier of *Steel Magnolias* in 1990 and again on an official visit to Korea in 1992. The dress is exquisite, breathtaking, and finer than anything any woman in generations of my family has ever hoped to own. And the mannequin, of course, is shaped precisely like Diana; no adjustments to the dresses have been made. Against my will, I feel a deep and painful twinge of envy. For the body of Diana, even headless, is voluptuous, perfectly proportioned.

We move on to subdued gown in ivory silk crepe, by Catherine

Walker, which Diana wore to a state banquet for the king and queen of Malaysia in 1993. Its simplicity only highlights the luxurious curves of Diana's body.

"Admit it, she was built," says Mom, so loud several other women turn around. "I mean without implants, or any other surgical procedures. She was a knockout."

I nod agreement but feel the stirrings of some ancient hatred. I was, after all, the great-great-granddaughter of potato farmers exiled during The Hunger. I had trouble filling an A cup.

"Of course, she was an aristocrat. So it's in the blood, that beauty." Mom nods to herself, as if she's just made an official pronouncement. Then she hobbles off toward the next dress, listing slightly toward the right.

Displayed are maybe twenty of Diana's castoffs, all sold for charity at the Christie's auction two months before she died. A copy of a letter, handwritten by Diana and enlarged umpteen times, credits William, the future king, with the idea of the auction. Mixed with the dresses are copies of mementos, like the letter, and full color photographs of Diana doing her charity work — holding hands with AIDS patients, hugging handicapped children, walking through a minefield in Angola. Like works of art, the dresses have titles and cards to describe them. Mounted next to many are gigantic news photos of the princess wearing them at public functions — state dinners, openings, fund-raisers. The photos are black and white, blurred like fading memories.

Several museum guards and a young Lowell cop — gun, badge and all — watch, circulating, reminders that the dresses are worth millions, may even have historical significance. Groups of women hover by the glass cases, linking arms. Most are well dressed in suits and pumps; they're manicured and coiffured. Mom and I are not among them. Jeans, a sweatshirt and running shoes were the best that I could manage. In the museum's reverential light, next to an off-the-shoulder number slit up to there, and aglow with sparkly beads, I notice a jam stain — Welch's grape — on the front of my sweatshirt. It looks exactly like Australia on my son's Montessori puzzle of the world. Must've happened when I was making the kids' sandwiches. I twist my fanny pack around to cover it.

As for Mom, she's wearing what has become her uniform: polyester pull-on pants (Wash and wear!), a matching print over blouse (Hides a multitude of sins!) and her Hush Puppy walkers in taupe (They're soooo comfy, and they go with everything!) Even her hair is drip dry, or at least towel dry, the kind of short frizzy perm that went out of fashion twenty years ago.

"Clothes horses," I sniff, nodding to the group in front of us, three anorexic women in Chanel type suits, and the kind of shoulder bag Diana favored. "Corporate wives with money and time to burn."

"Don't knock it until you've tried it," says Mom. "Anyway, they're wearing copies, not the real thing."

"Since when did you become an expert in high fashion?"

"One of the many interests I've developed in my dotage," she answers.

"Watching the home shopping channels?"

"Nah," she says. "They don't sell *haute couture*."

She pronounces *haute* as hot. I don't bother to correct her. We try to go through the exhibit sedately, like the well-heeled matrons who surround us. But we're bedazzled, hungry to see everything but unable to absorb it. We lurch among "Midi-Length Evening Dress" in white silk chiffon with pearlized sequins; "Long Dinner Dress" in dark green silk velvet; "Long Dress for Scottish Dancing," which has a fitted bodice of black velvet over a voluminous plaid silk skirt.

"Now we're talking turkey," says my fashion expert mother when looking at another dress by Walker which, the card tells us, was worn by Diana on her India Tour in 1992. "Now this is truly regal. Jesus."

The billowing skirt is made of fine pink silk, but the bodice and short fitted jacket are embroidered with white and green sequins shaped like flowers, glass beads, and gold braid. They card says a team of needlewomen work full-time for a month to complete it.

Among the gowns, like that one, worn for public occasions, are several 'worn for private functions only', a nautical style evening dress with one sleeve; a sarong style gown encrusted with pearls and sequins.

"What kind of private function do you figure?" I ask Mom. I'm fantasizing cocktails with the queen; dinner at the palace with a few members of the aristocracy, the ladies in waiting.

"Don't need clothes like this for any private functions I know of," Mom cackles. "They'd really cramp my style."

I lose Mom for a few minutes, and lose myself in the forest of regal garments. I pause at a long-sleeved burgundy gown with a gargantuan bow upon the derriere, worn to the Back to the Future premier in 1985. I'm wondering how Diana could have concentrated on Michael J. Fox while sitting on this big bow when I sense a commotion, see Mom up ahead leaning against a glass case, one palm pressed flat against it. Her right arm appears to have gone limp, and her cane is tilted sideways, the roots pulled from the earth. I rush toward her. A cardiovascular event, maybe the big one, I'm thinking. The cop reaches her first.

"Do you need help? A wheelchair?" He is touching Mom's elbow, helping her to right herself. I see that she's been looking at the John Travolta, the elegant silk velvet like the one on the Diana doll she owns.

"I'm fine, fine," she says, pulling herself up to her full height, five feet even, though she swears that she's been shrinking. She grasps her cane with both hands, reattaching the roots. Her cheeks are wet with tears.

"Did you know," she asks the cop, "did you know she was butt naked in the morgue in France? Dodi's dad, el Fayed, that crook, took off with all her clothes, and they had nothing to put on her to send her body home. Did you know?"

"We have a wheelchair if you need it," says the cop. "Otherwise, don't touch the glass."

Mom gives him her Look, that of despot, a potentate, the one with which she makes her daughters quake. The cop shrugs and walks away.

"You scared the crap out of me." I try whispering, but it comes out more like a hiss.

"They had to borrow a dress from the wife of the president of France," she says, wiping her cheeks with one hand. "A plain black sheath, two sizes too small. They couldn't even zipper it."

"I thought you were having a stroke." I'm hissing even louder, but she looks away, waves her hand at me, the mimed version of MYOB.

We stay for a few minutes in front of the John Travolta. We look at the gown and then at the photographs of the radiant Diana and Travolta dancing, the Reagans and Prince Charles in the back ground smiling. Again I feel a stab of jealousy—over Diana's beauty, her great body, her wealth and celebrity; her glamorous life. But as I feel this, I also think, Hey, wait, I'm alive, she isn't. Even with my meager breasts, my messy kitchen, and my mortgage; my noisy kids and depressed mother, the jam stain on my sweatshirt. I'm alive, she isn't. I'm seized by an insane urge to shout and whoop when Mom interrupts.

"She had the right idea, dying young and beautiful."

"Oh, Mom." I grab her shoulder, shake her. "Diana didn't want to die. A fatal crash wasn't in her five-year plan."

"Maybe not," Mom murmurs, but she doesn't sound convinced.

After this, she's had enough. She turns down my offer of cappuccino and biscotti in the museum's coffee bar. She wants to get home for one of her shows. I walk her to the bench outside, tell her to wait while I get the car, but she pulls me down beside her. Sitting close, I hear a slight, phlegmy rattle.

"After I go," she says, "you kids can go through my closets and drawers and gather up my finest things. Drape them on some headless mannequins and tell the story of my life."

I look at her.

"Black polyester pull-on pants and matching jungle print big top worn to Senior's Bingo at Our Lady Queen of Peace, 1999."

"Yeah, okay," I answer, catching on. "Navy mail order pull-ons with matching cardigan over nautical print T-shirt. Worn in August, to North Shore Radiologic, for an MRI scan of the brain."

"And again, on a shopping trip to Wal-Mart."

"What were you buying, Mom? On the shopping trip. We should say. Maybe have a photograph. Enlarged."

"Denture cleaner. Depends."

"Not yet. Not either one."

"Won't be long now," she answers. Yet she's smiling, and she seems, for this one small moment, to have misplaced her anger, her ill health, her disappointments.

"Don't charge admission, though," she says. "Let everybody in for free."

I almost choke on laughter. Who, I wonder, does she think will come? I envision the hordes jostling for admission to Diana's Dresses but hardly anyone for Mom: me and my sisters; our husbands and kids, a neighbor or two, maybe Daddy if he's not too busy.

"Make it a freebie," Mom repeats, riffling through her waistpack for a smoke. "Promise you'll let everyone in for free."

"Sure, Mom, no problem," I say, going along with her parody that faceless throngs, maybe an SRO crowd, would be vying for the chance to see her stuff. I get up, stifling exasperation as she takes out yet another cigarette. "If it's your last wish, we'll be happy to honor it."

Then I take off, heading for the car, and I hear or think I hear the click and hiss of her Bic and smell her smoky exhalation.

WEAPONS OF WAR

THE MORNING'S COLD AND STILL, the sky streaked gray and orange, heavy with the promise of more snow. Helen wakes up in the cool gray light, disoriented from a dream, groggy from the cocktails and wines she'd drunk the day before. Christmas dinner at her sister's. What was the dream? It's gone but she feels its bitter, unsettling aftermath. Helen heaves herself out from under the down comforter, slides her feet into sheepskin slippers on the floor next to the bed. So much to do today, but first things first. She pulls a sweatshirt on over her flannel pajamas. Showing David who's the boss. Who's in charge. Who runs this little family. She shivers as she stumbles downstairs for coffee, steaming in the electric percolator she set with a timer the night before, its lovely smell wafting up the stairs. Most mornings, Helen treasures the first quiet moments of the day, alone with her coffee and her thoughts.

But today, the day after Christmas, 1975, she hears noises in the living room. Looks into the big room off the hallway. Sees that already, at 6:45 a.m., a search and destroy mission is in progress. The barrel of an assault rifle points at her from behind the club chair.

Then she sees him, David, her son, her beloved only child, ooching on his belly, across the carpet, an imitation Aubuisson, bought at Sears the year before. Camouflage over his pajamas. Netted helmet on his head. Grenades and knives dragging on his hips as he slithers across the rug. Nothing on his feet. His soles, from this perspective, are soft and pink, like an exotic summer fruit. When he was a baby, still in diapers, Helen, after changing him, sometimes clapped his feet together to make him laugh, then, making loud smooching sounds, kissed his toes, one by one

David, grunting and heaving in combat against imagined enemies, hasn't noticed Helen in the doorway. Just beyond him, in one corner, is their Christmas tree, decorated entirely with ornaments she and David have made: Popcorn garlands. Waxed paper snowflakes edged with silver glitter. Construction paper angels. Clothespin reindeer. She recalls David's delight, the day before, when he opened his gifts, full battle gear, from her father, Papa John. The whole family had been invited to her sister Leona's home — Helen, a single parent, the black sheep, had only recently been allowed back into the fold. How precarious she'd felt, as if with one wrong word, one false move, she'd be lost forever. David tore through his packages like a lunatic, whooping and hollering when he first put on the helmet and the jacket. The little soldier man. After that, the awful rat-a-tat-tat of the plastic gun; David's crazed laugh every time he pretended to have killed someone.

Watching David slide behind the couch, Helen recalls her father watching his grandchildren, not just David, but David and his cousins, a half dozen of them, watching with intense pleasure and pride as the boys crawled and staggered past the Christmas tree, between the chairs and sofas, and finally out onto the snowy lawn.

The grown-ups had gathered with their cocktails before a roaring fire in Leona's elegant living room, newly redone, with its gleaming Ethan Allen furniture. Some European choir was singing carols in the background. Through the big bay window, the grown-ups watched the children sniping at each other from behind the tall pin oaks, lobbing their grenades from foxholes in the shrubs, and finally engaging in hand-to-hand combat, wrestling and stabbing one another in the snow.

Watching David, intent upon his mission, Helen feels again the outrage she'd felt the day before, the wrongness of it all, the grown-ups, luxuriating in prosperity, encouraging the children in their war games. Wretched violence, no reason, no justification for it. At Leona's, sipping a Manhattan from a crystal tumbler, its heat cascading into her belly, Helen had cried out, 'Doesn't anyone remember?' Body bags, zipped up, heaved onto air transports, hundreds of them, some containing boys they'd gone to high school with. Enemy dead. Kill ratios. Then, just last April, after rivers of blood and death, capitulation, the abandonment of Saigon, the terrified rush to the embassy roof, the horror.

"Doesn't anyone remember?" was all Helen said, but Leona, nine years older, turned to her. 'Don't start that stuff here,' she said. 'Not now. It's not appropriate.' Helen's father had said nothing, but he'd given her the look, an icy stare that even now, at her age, scared her. There'd been a moment of awful silence, then another carol had begun, *God rest ye merry gentlemen*. Outside, the children went on with their game, their wild cries piercing the French doors, the elaborate velvet drapery. Helen went to the bar to pour herself another drink. Nothing Santa Claus had brought David — an electronic keyboard, a set of expensive pastels, a pup tent and sleeping bag — could rival his gifts from Papa John.

Helen doesn't interrupt David, but instead pads into the kitchen where she makes them French toast with butter, the last of the maple syrup they'd bought on a trip to Vermont that fall. With the French toast on the griddle, she goes to the living room to tell David breakfast is ready. 'I'm starving,' David hollers from his combat zone. Helen puts Streisand's Christmas Album on the stereo in the living room, turns the volume loud enough for them to hear in the kitchen. 'Take that stuff off before coming to the table,' she commands and David obeys without complaint. At the table, between bites, David sings along with Streisand in his pure sweet voice. *Jingle bells, jingle bells, jingle all the way.* Listening to him hum, watching him, a wad of French toast in his cheek, a fleck of syrup on his chin, Helen ponders what his music teacher recently told her about him: that he had perfect pitch; that he was gifted with an astonishing musicality. Her exact words. Gifted.

When they finish eating, she tells David to get dressed. To gather up his guns and his grenades. All of his new war stuff from Papa John. She dresses herself in jeans and work boots, collects trash bags full of Christmas wrappings. Shoves them into the trunk of her Datsun.

"Where we going, Mom? What's up?" David asks, over and over, as she drives the empty back roads to the landfill. "You'll see." Irritated, unable to say more. The shoulders of the road are clotted with muddied snow but in the distance, the wooded hills glisten pearly white.

Helen drives David to the landfill where they dump their trash every other week. The watchman waves as Helen drives through the chain link gate. She turns along the gravel road that will bring her to the dump's most distant reach. The landfill is a series of peaks and valleys, vast and bleak. Smoldering here and there with small, stinking fires. Black streaks waft to the sky, now patched here and there with pink. Like broiled salmon, Helen thinks, or peonies crushed on tarmac.

They pass scavengers gleaning treasures from rough slopes. Helen has done it herself. Once, she unearthed a trove of scarred rock maple furniture — bureau, bed, desk, chair. Vintage 40s stuff. She'd taken them home, stripped and refinished them for David's room.

"It isn't trash day, Mom. What's going on?" David kicks the seat with the back of one foot, then the other. His movement jounces Helen.

"You'll see."

She hates the tremor in his voice. Knows he's worried, but hasn't yet figured out what she's going to do. Knows he is incapable of imagining what she's about to do.

Helen stops at the far end of the landfill. Gets out, walks up the nearest slope. The peak she's standing on is a kind of cliff. The landfill falls away sharply at her feet. Far below, front loaders manipulate heaps of trash, forever changing the dump's dreary topography. Paper diapers, milk cartons, beer bottles, broken chairs, a bathtub, a Christmas tree or two — arrayed as far as she can see. Helen decides David must be the one to throw the guns onto the heap.

"Come on up here and bring your war stuff," she calls in her most soothing voice, a voice that won't give anything away.

Years later, when David calls to tell Helen that he has dropped out of the music program at Boston University, and enlisted in the army, of course, she will remember this day at the landfill. The day after Christmas, 1975. The day she made David throw away his guns. After David's call, Helen will see this incident as if it had happened just the day before: the two of them, in gray light, standing at the precipice above the trash. Will recall the rancid smell, the smell of smoke. Will watch them as if watching a film without its soundtrack: Mother towering over son. Leaning over to grab son's shoulders. Shaking him. Again and again. So hard his brain must be slamming against his skull. He must be seeing stars. His face streaked with tears, like a sidewalk after rain

When this event actually occurs, the soundtrack is high-pitched, shrill; the volume high enough for everyone to hear. "Bring the guns over here," Helen shouts again to David, who lingers by the Datsun's door. Holding on to his toys. "And the grenades. Bring them up here."

David shakes his head no, takes a step away from the car.

"Bring them up here now."

Again he shakes his head, takes another step away. She rushes toward him, lunges at him as he takes off, running with the guns. A panicked beast, he heads the wrong way, up along the landfill's ridge. She chases him. Overtakes him when he trips on something. Ornate leg of an old table. Walnut. Art deco. They sprawl amid the rubble. Ashy dust spills over them.

"They're mine. Papa John gave them to me." David shrieking, sobbing. "To me. They're mine." Mores shrieks and sobs. Helen's heart congeals. She stands, drags David to his feet. Shakes him, demands that he release the guns.

"Daddy was wrong, completely wrong to give them to you," she cries. Voice operatic, echoing among the peaks and valleys of the dump. "He didn't have the right. Knowing how I feel."

"Mine. They're mine."

"When you grow up and have your own house, your own

family, you can do anything you want. You can have anything you want. But I'm the grown-up now. This is my family. And I won't have guns in my house."

"Toys. They're just toys. And they're mine."

She grabs at the guns, clasped with ferocious strength in David's arms, against his chest. Tugs with all her strength. Stumbles backward when the plastic barrel of the M-16 snaps off. Helen stands there with the broken barrel, feeling that something vital has just broken between them. Doesn't understand it. Jabs him in the chest with the broken barrel.

"Someday you'll understand." The bottom of her belly quivers, pushing out this sound.

"I'll never understand a witch like you. No I won't. I won't ever understand."

She steps up to the precipice. Hurls the broken pieces of the M-16 over the side. Stomps back to him.

"Go get the rest of the stuff." Voice bubbling in her throat like a corrosive fluid. David shakes his head no. Clamps his arms across his chest as she goes for the submachine gun.

"I could shake the living daylights out of you!"

She is shaking now herself. Pulls the submachine gun free. Rushes up the slope, tosses it over.

"If you hate me so much, why don't you throw me into the trash too?"

"I don't hate you. I hate guns."

"They're toys! They're mine."

"Weapons of war are not appropriate playthings. In my opinion. And my opinion is the only one that matters."

Now Helen drags David back to the Datsun. Makes him pick

up the grenades, the rubber knives, the bayonet, the flak jacket, the netted helmet, all scattered on the floor, the front bucket seats. This effort takes forever because David keeps going limp. Passive resistance, like a protester collapsing before riot geared police. After his third or fourth collapse —she loses count —Helen smacks him on his bottom, his back, something she has never done before. She feels her palm enflamed. Feels herself white-hot, incandescent with rage. Glimpses, for an instant, David's helplessness. Sees she's crushed him. Stripped him of his power. She glows now with triumph, pulsing like a neon sign. Wishes her own father were there to see. Daddy. Papa John. Who had no right to give David gifts like these.

Helen catches her breath. Counts to nine. In what she considers an expression of great generosity, tells David he may keep the flashlight and the canteen.

"I don't want that crap," he says.

"Have it your way."

She pulls him by the arm back up the slope. Makes him stand beside her as she throws the rubber knives, the grenades, the flashlight, the camouflage canteen. David's blood-curdling scream roils and echoes through smoky hills and valleys.

"I hate you. I hate you, you old witch. You stupid thing."

Helen pretends she cannot hear him. Follows the toys' trajectory. Sees them hit the slope and slide into a smoky valley.

"I hate you. I wish you weren't my mother. I wish I wasn't born."

The scavengers are moving closer. Helen sees them pause to watch. Figures, as soon as she and David leave, the scavengers will come after the guns, grenades, flak jacket, netted helmet. Figures they will take them. Give them to their own children. Or sell them to other children at a nearby flea market. Decides it doesn't matter. Doesn't matter that her son's discarded war toys will be recycled to other children. What matters is that she made her point. Made her point with David. Now he knows her values. Knows what she means when she says that she's a pacifist. Not just opposed to war but also to the glorification of military might.

David's sobs are deep, metronomic, as Helen drags him back to the Datsun. His chest and shoulders jerk. "One and a half million Vietnamese were killed during the war," she tells him. Voice exhausted, toneless. "Fifty thousand American soldiers, too. One of them your father."

David's sobbing ends abruptly with a hiccup. The light in his eyes goes out as if she'd flipped a switch.

Later that day Helen took David to McDonald's for a Happy Meal that did not make him happy. Then to the movies— ET? She couldn't remember. He hadn't liked that either. He let his ice cream Bon-Bons melt inside their cardboard carton. During the forgotten film, Helen experienced severe, if premature, hot flashes. Scalding waves of remorse, chagrin. But she couldn't find a way to tell him.

After the movie and McDonald's, she let David, with his Christmas money, buy a wood-carving kit. What he liked best about this kit was the glittering little knife. Later he would fashion handguns and bows and arrows with this knife. Primitive weapons, but no mistaking what they were. Later still, Helen will decide, all things considered, that the homemade toys, utilizing as they did his imagination, and his fine motor skills, were not as harmful, or as morally repugnant, as the expensive and gruesomely realistic G.I. Joe versions. The day after Christmas 1975. David, six. Helen, 24.

Though David spent that Christmas vacation in a pink-cheeked snit, mostly hiding in his room, holding onto his anger longer than Helen had imagined possible, he never again asked to buy a gun. He even told his friends, when inviting them to his birthday parties, that he was not allowed to play with guns. Helen overheard him once, and she'd been so proud.

When he was 13, on one of his many sleep overs at his grandfather's, David left behind a pair of boots. Sometime later, searching for these boots when her father wasn't home, Helen found a toy box in the guest room closet, the room where David stayed. She flipped the lid, thinking the boots might be inside. What she found instead was an arsenal. Plastic Uzis, M-16s. Bazookas. Bayonets. Grenades. A complete set of G.I. Joe camouflage gear in a size David had surely outgrown. Folded neatly next to it was the real thing, purchased from a local military surplus store, the tags still on. All in a size David would just be growing into. Netted helmet. Flak jacket. Ammo belt.

NATIVITY

JUDY O'GRADY WAKES UP QUIVERING like a tuning fork in the bottom bunk of a room she shares with two of her five sisters. She sits up, careful to avoid hitting her head on the wood slats of the bunk above her. Hunched in the dark, breathless, she feels the baby move, the touch of a feather. It would be easy to ignore, the way she's been ignoring all the other symptoms for so many weeks. But then she feels it again, a faint but persistent signal, like a fingertip traced lightly down her forearm. It's what has awakened her, this feathery touch. Her dreams wove themselves around it and then she saw the baby, arms outstretched, trying to wake her up.

Quickening, Judy knows that's the word. Quickening. She wonders, vaguely, about the roots of it. Quick was the most tender part of human flesh, like under your fingernail. Hurt to the quick. Feeling the baby move.

With her sister Jacqueline sound asleep above her and her sister Julianne in a bed across the room, their breathing synchronous, steady as a heartbeat, Judy places her palms on her belly and feels it jump, and then again, a strong, deep movement. In the dark, against the breathing of her sisters, she imagines her baby, a small swimmer, splashing and flailing in its amniotic bubble. Her heart begins to misfire, clutching and slamming in her chest. Judy reaches over to the bedside table and shuts off the alarm before it rings. Today's the day she'll tell her parents. She will have to tell them. No alternatives exist. Even the women she works with seem suspicious, eyeing her belly, joking about her constant hunger. But Judy doesn't know how to tell her parents. She can't say the words out loud, not to Mata Hari and J. Edgar Hoover. Judy has trouble telling them she's going to the movies, or the library; that she has a toothache or needs new glasses. How can she tell them she's pregnant? She can't. She can't say the words out loud to her mother and father any more than she can say them to herself. She knows she'll shrivel in their gaze, transform into a desiccated sac of skin and bone.

For the longest time, weeks and weeks, ever since flunking out of the university her freshman year, Judy couldn't even think the word pregnant. She couldn't think pregnant or any of its variations, in a family way, bun in the oven, knocked up, with child, not even in her most unguarded moments, as when she's drifting off to sleep at night. The reality was beyond her, that a viable fetus gestated within her, just south of her bellybutton and north of her pubic bone. Instead, since returning from the university, Judy has lived in a state of soft unfeeling, pierced only by her great hunger. She is always sneaking food, candy bars, cookies, lunch meat, fruit; hiding food in her pockets and her drawers except at work where she can eat anything she wants, all day, and nobody cares. Nobody says anything.

Since coming home, she has seen no one except her sisters. She does nothing except sleep, read, eat and go to work. Once in a while she makes false entries in her journal, a marble composition book she knows her mother reads. She'll make up existential babble or copy a passage from Camus, and hide the journal between her mattress and box spring. For her mother's reading pleasure.

Through much of the spring and half the summer, Judy had waited for the beloved, if ancient and forgetful hound, her period. She understood that its absence signaled merely a temporary disorientation, a glitch in the position of the moon. Soon the hound would find its way home. Several times she strapped on a pad from the gigantic store brand box she and her sisters shared, comforted by the familiar lump between her legs and certain that by day's end, the red stain would appear. Judy kept taking pads, one by one, and discarding them, unused, in the trash at work because she knew her mother checked such things. Her mother counted the pads.

Several times during those weeks, when she was vomiting every morning, Judy saw traces of red, tiny blood streaks on her panties, and she tamped down her jubilation. She understood that the hound was back on track, faithful, and making its slow way back to her. But nothing happened. Despite its spoor, the hound never appeared. Then she felt the baby move.

It is 1968, the summer that came after the Summer of Love, and Judy is working at a box factory two and a half miles from her family's home in southwestern Massachusetts. There she punches a time clock and earns piece work rates. This morning she gets up, rummages through a drawer for a pair of shorts and cotton shirt, two of the last things she owns that still fit. The waistband pinches and she knows that before the day is through, she'll unbutton the top button and the first half-inch of zipper, hiding them beneath her shirttail.

Judy gets up and leaves for work extra early because she doesn't want to see her parents, not today or any other day. Mata Hari and J. Edgar Hoover are her secret names for them, names she'd given them in high school, Mata and J. Edgar, names so secret she wouldn't even share them with her sisters; M.H. and Hoover, a fun couple. If Judy manages to avoid them in the morning before she leaves, she won't have to see them till supper, and, after that, for just a couple of hours before she collapses, exhausted, into bed.

Just before 6:30 a.m., hardly awake, but grateful that, at last, she doesn't throw up first thing after opening her eyes, Judy leaves the house. She carries a brown bag lunch she's fixed the night before — tuna sandwich, Fritos and peanut butter cookies, a paperback copy of Camus' The Stranger in French, covered in a brown wrapper she's fashioned from a grocery bag, and money for breakfast and snacks throughout the day. From her neighborhood in the hills above the town, tiered streets lined with well kept Victorian and Colonial style homes, Judy heads down through the town center to the box factory on its outskirts. All day — four hours in the morning, an hour for lunch, four more in the afternoon — Judy O'Grady sits on a high stool at a long table with a dozen other women, most middle-aged, many grandmothers. The women put together velvet boxes that will eventually hold rosary beads, expensive ones of sterling silver, amber, pearl, aurora borealis. While she works, Judy imagines them, profusions of glistening semi-precious stones attached in precise patterns and completed by the elaborate sterling or gold-plated crucifix, Christ on the cross. Christ who died to give us all eternal life. She imagines families like her own, parents and children, on their knees praying the rosary together, the glorious, sorrowful and joyful mysteries, the beads shimmering between their pressed palms. *The family that prays together stays together,* Hoover always claimed. Declaimed. But the women on the line never got to see the beads in the boxes unless they looked for them in stores. At work, they pass the boxes along the table, each completing some small task. Judy's is to insert with hot glue the pastel satin linings. She doesn't seem to notice her fingers are covered with blisters and burn scars. The other women believe she has a high tolerance for pain.

Sometimes, while working, Judy whispers to herself the mysteries just to see if she can still remember them in the right order — the Annunciation, the Visitation, the Nativity, the Finding in the Temple; the Agony in the Garden, the Scourging at the Pillar, the Crowning with Thorns, the Carrying of the Cross, the Crucifixion; the Resurrection, the Ascension, the Descent of the Holy Spirit. The Agony in the Garden was Judy's favorite. No matter how you looked at it, as far as mysteries went, it was tough to beat. The Agony in the Garden

In a line along the center of the table are the various hand tools, scissors and pliers, the women use to make the boxes, along with small framed photos of their children and grandchildren: birth, First Communion, prom and graduation pictures. Three black plastic ashtrays are set equidistant from each other among the personal mementos, though the women, when they're smoking, tend to move the ashtrays closer to themselves. The ashtrays are clean and shiny every morning at 7:30 when the starting bell rings; heaped with crushed smoldering butts — Marlboros, Luckies, Newports, Pall Malls — by lunch break. Judy doesn't smoke. All day she sits inhaling others' smoke, her eyes and nostrils stinging.

J. Edgar, known to the rest of the world as Joe O'Grady, had gotten Judy this job through a friend of his in the Altar and

Aesthetics Society at Our Lady Queen of Peace. After she flunked out of the university, earning no credit whatsoever second semester, wasting thousands of his hard-earned dollars, and showing no appreciation whatsoever for how hard he'd worked for her, for her future. Time she got a taste of the real world, he said. Learned how it felt to earn an honest buck, not posing for dirty pictures. *I never posed for dirty pictures,* Judy cried, indignant. *I modeled for life classes in the art department. Art's my major. Everyone takes turns.*

This argument, one in an endless series, took place in the kitchen after all the other girls were in bed. It started after Mata, a.k.a. Maeve O'Grady, on one of her snooping expeditions through Judy's things, found some rolled up drawings in the closet, drawings Judy's classmates had given her: Judy posing supine on a couch, her nipples erect, her hand draped across one hip, fingertips touching her pubis.

Judy sat, hunched over, on a stool beneath the kitchen's hideous fluorescent light, in the hideous kitchen, with its hideous yellow countertops and shiny pine cabinets, the place she hated more than any other in the world, and the place J. Edgar favored for his interrogations, his torture sessions. Judy couldn't remember all the times she'd been here, in this same spot, her father shouting, flailing, threatening one thing or another. She did not want to remember. That night, the night of the discovered drawings, he waved the rolled up drawings like a wand, but Judy did not disappear.

Art, cried Judy, *art.*

But J. Edgar said nude was nude in front of all those people, and he smacked her, back-handed on one cheek, and pounded her head with the drawings in his other hand. Judy's mother Maeve, Mata, sat at the kitchen table, watching with no expression, not exactly looking at her daughter, but maybe at the vast mystifying space that seemed to surround her.

Naked before the multitudes. My own daughter, J. Edgar continued. *Making a flagrant display of herself, defying all that the Holy Mother stands for. Just like in a peep show, like in the Combat Zone.* Then he ignited the drawings with the gas flame of the stove, held them over the kitchen sink until the flame threatened his fingers, dropped them into the sink, and turned on the faucet. A hissing plume of steam arose. Mata Hari sat and watched, not making a sound. Read the lives of the saints, he said once the drawings had turned to ash, and he handed her a copy.

After that, he declared it was time, no, way past time, that Judy began to earn her keep, and he gave her the details of the job she would begin in the morning. Now every other Friday, when Judy gets her pay envelope — cash, with a handwritten tally of her hours and her piecework — J. Edgar waits in the kitchen for her to hand it over. With a flourish, he hands her back a $20, warning her to spend it wisely; it had to last two weeks. Then he turns to Mata and winks, sharing a joke Judy did not understand. The rest of her paycheck he put toward Judy's debt to him, the thousands she had wasted at the university.

At one end of the long factory table a black and silver RCA radio is tuned to a pop station out of Boston that features Frank Sinatra, Steve and Eydie, Tony Bennett. The women keep the volume low so as not to disturb workers at other tables, where they make different kinds of boxes, and have their own radios tuned to their own stations. *If you're going to San Francisco ...* It's enough to make Judy want to puke even if she isn't, at the moment, nauseous.

Judy is completing her 17th box of the day, hot glue oozing from the edges, stinging her thumbs, when she hits upon the idea of a letter. Right away, she realizes that writing to her parents is the perfect solution. That way, she can tell them the entire awful truth, and they'll be able to read it, absorb it, in their own time. They won't be able to start screaming at her, making fun of her or hitting her. They can read it, talk about it with each other, then respond. Judy doesn't, can't, dwell too much on this last part, their response. When she does, she gets an awful feeling, one she can't explain or describe, but much worse than the nausea. Judy begins composing the letter in her mind, creating a small quiet place within the factory's cacophony, the machines, the radios, the hum of many, many voices; several kinds of whistles and alarms, the clanking of the time clock not far from where she sits.

I've felt so lost. I haven't known where to turn. Please help me. I have sinned. I am sinful and sorrowful. Yes, me, your prodigal daughter. I look ahead and I'm so scared. I don't know what will happen, or how I will get through this. I don't know how or why it happened ...

This thought pulls back a curtain and Judy, picking spilled glue off her fingertips, glimpses someone who looks exactly like herself, only thinner, happier, wrapped in a gilded shawl, leaping and pirouetting in a meadow beneath a domed and starry sky. Not far from the gilded dancer, sitting cross-legged in the grass, is a long lean boy named Bobby and he's playing the harmonica, something bluesy, a composition of his own. The notes spill out like water, swirling around them. Bobby's long hair fails across his face, shimmering, and the girl pauses in her dance to touch it, to smooth it back so she can see his face, his beautiful face. Then Judy can't watch anymore.

I don't know how it happened. Judy, reaching for another box, repeats this phrase, as if to convince herself. *I know things haven't gone well between us for these past few years. You hate my painting. I know that. Plus, you're always comparing us, me and Jacqueline and Julianne. You point out all the things that are right with them and wrong with me.*

By accident, Judy snaps shut a box on her own fingers. She winces from the pain. She won't ever write her parents such a letter, that she knows. She can't even decide upon a salutation. Dear Mom and Dad ... Dear Mother and Father ... Dear Mommy and Daddy ... Dearest Parents ... Dear Maeve and Joe...

This last one cracks Judy up, and she laughs out loud. The women on the line turn to look at her, eyebrows raised. They appear to want an explanation, but Judy remains mute, her face enflamed. She grabs the next box, ignoring their soft laughter. She hardly ever addresses either of her parents directly, hardly ever calls them Mom and Dad, or Mother and Father. She can't remember the last time, and the names feel foreign when she whispers them to herself. Judy prefers her own names for them, Mata Hari and J. Edgar, but she reminds herself that she's stopping all of that, the sarcasm, the irony, the bitter jokes to herself. M.H. and Hoover were about to be cast into the dustbin of history, a phrase she'd learned in a European history class she flunked.

Later that evening, at home, hiding in her bedroom, Judy scribbles this note, then puts it into an envelope inside her marble composition book, which she wedges back between the mattress and box spring, knowing her mother will find it on one of her reconnaissance missions.

Dear Mom and Dad,

I think I've waited too long to tell you this. I'm pregnant. I really don't know how it happened. But that's it. Yours truly, with child.

Judy

Today, Maeve O'Grady drives Judy out to the edge of town, out past the churches, the pharmacies and funeral homes of the sprawling New England suburb, past the factories, and the hunched gray paint works with their spuming furnaces. Maeve is behind the wheel of the white Chevy station wagon, a nine-seater, bought off the lot at an end-of-season sale, one year earlier. The red plastic upholstery stings through the cotton of Judy's loose fitting muumuu, one she's sewn from a Simplicity pattern out of flowered cotton. The windows are rolled down and the dusty August heat swirls around the women as they speed out of town.

Maeve taps the gas in an odd syncopated rhythm as if keeping time to music only she can hear. The radio is not turned on. She squints into the light, her cheeks flushed, her fingers thrumming. Now and then she lets go of the steering wheel, and her fingers stretch out straight as though she's gesticulating, maybe teaching a lesson. But she doesn't speak. For this task, she has fortified herself with Gilbey's gin and orange juice, an effective medicinal, or so she tells herself.

Judy turned 19 not long before, though she is, with her angular face and haughty manner, often mistaken for someone older. Right now, pallid and exhausted, she fights nausea and the weight of her eyelids is too much to bear. She lets them close, her face go slack, her head bob upon her neck in a way certain to irritate her mother.

Maeve O'Grady, not yet forty, is still slim and pretty, 'a good lookin' gal', Daddy says, youthful, in spite of having borne so many children, a brood of six daughters, every one of whom she hoped would be a boy. Hardly anyone who meets Maeve and Judy alone together ever guesses correctly their relationship, a situation that ceased to surprise them long ago. For Maeve and Judy, mother and daughter, often look at one another without recognition, without seeing anything familiar, anything understandable. Neither has the words to solve this mystery, but the words go with them anyway, a nimbus muffling everything they say to one another. Now everything they haven't spoken to each other is there between them on the red plastic seat of the Chevy station wagon as they speed out of town, and the unspoken words have weight and mass, not unlike a toxic gas.

Maeve drives out the hilly back roads to the Fox Hollow Country Club of which the O'Gradys are not members. The Fox Hollow Country Club for which J. Edgar has naught but scorn, and Mata agrees with him completely. But the Fox Hollow Country Club, with its multiple swimming pools, cabanas, tennis courts; its verdant, pristine golf course, its restaurants and bars, is known to them. It is always there, in their dreams and memories, a beckoning life beyond their reach. Maeve pulls over onto the grassy shoulder. The high curved gates of Fox Hollow glisten just ahead. A sugar maple, in the rich foliage of a hot, wet summer, curves its limbs toward them but Maeve overshoots the shade. She and Judy end up in the blinding light, the shadows of the maple dancing on the seat behind them. In front of them, in miniature, on the rolling green hills of the golf course, they see men and women golfing among their caddies and their carts, taking swings, chasing balls, laughing and chatting with each other.

Maeve and Judy could become transfixed, eventually forget what they were doing here. Sitting in the Chevy watching, the windows rolled down so that they hear, as if from another galaxy, the muted shouts and laughter of the golfers.

"I'm so ashamed of you," says Maeve, at last, looking through the windshield glittering with refracted light. Her words come out in a peculiar hiss as if from a leaking inflatable device. "Everything we've given you. You've had every advantage."

Judy rouses herself to listen. She prickles at her mother's words. Ashamed. This is not the script she had imagined.

"The first chance you get, you go and ruin our name, our family's name. You're the kind of child who makes me wish I were not a mother. I'm so ashamed. Of you. For you."

A bee has made its way into the car. It seems to be stuck at the intersection of the dashboard and windshield, just below the inspection sticker, on the driver's side. It buzzes desperately, its wings fluttering, its antennae arching. You make me wish I weren't a mother. So ashamed. No. Not at all.

"But I should have figured. You've always been a troublemaker. A tramp. With your weird friends and your secrets."

Now Judy sits up taller, turns to look at her mother. She'd imagined making contact, eye contact, something. Maybe what she wanted, though she never could have said it, was for her mother to acknowledge her, to admit her into the world of grown-up women. She didn't dare hope but couldn't help longing for some kind of breakthrough, a shattering of the invisible, protective shield that seemed always to surround them, in separate bubbles. Judy watches her mother clutching the red steering wheel, leaning toward the windshield as if trying to see the golfers better.

"Everything Daddy and I have worked for. Everything we've wanted for you kids."

"Look at that bee," says Judy, wondering how it could be so dumb, wedging itself into that place, impossible to escape from.

"Pay attention, damn you," Maeve shouts, clutching the wheel tighter, like the car was still in motion. It's all she can do not to reach over and hit Judy, to wring her neck. "Of course, now I realize I should have known. But you've always had a problem with your weight. I just figured you were getting fat again. The way you were packing it on. Do any of your clothes still fit?"

This question slithers through Judy, but she doesn't answer. No, her clothes no longer fit. She has already outgrown them all. She can't help it. She's always hungry. She eats and eats, but never feels quite full.

"Don't expect us to be buying new ones for you. Not when you've eaten yourself out of an entire wardrobe."

An entire wardrobe, Judy snorts to herself. A couple of pairs of shorts and T-shirts off the clearance rack at Sears & Roebuck, her father's favorite store. Hand-me-downs from her older sister, her cousins.

"Well, you'll have to leave," Maeve continues, words she seems to have rehearsed, so measured, no feeling behind them. "You can't live with us." She shakes her head, as though she is looking at her daughter instead of distant golfers. "That's what Daddy said. You're the bad apple. You have to be removed from the basket."

A shrill sound — a bark, a snort — erupts from Judy, she can't control it, and now Maeve lets her have it, striking her backhanded, the prongs of her engagement diamond strafing Judy's lips, nose, cheek.

"What's so goddamned funny?" Maeve cries as Judy grabs her face, stinging from the slap. Her question reaches Judy on fumes of Gilbeys, but she doesn't recognize the smell.

"Who's the father?" Maeve asks now. "Tell me who the father is. He has to take some responsibility. That's what Daddy said."

Judy sits, holding the answer to this question, a wild card, in her mind, her heart. She wonders, but only vaguely, when and how to play it. She thinks about the boy again, the boy who disappeared, taking with him a big chunk of her heart, and leaving behind the baby fluttering in her womb.

"Who? Who?" Mother repeats, reminding Judy of an owl joke she'd heard ages before.

"I don't know, I'm not sure," Judy hears herself say. She has played the card in a way she hadn't planned, putting it out there, almost against her own will. "I don't know who the father is."

"Get out. Get out right now." Maeve presses her forehead against the steering wheel, ending the longest conversation she's had with Judy in at least four years. "I can't stand the sight of you. Find your own way home."

Judy climbs out of the Chevy and stands for a moment in the hot shade of the big maple. She watches her mother pull a U-turn, tires screeching, and head back to town.

Maeve and Joe O'Grady make an appointment for their daughter with an OB/gyn in Boston, a physician recommended to them by Father Leonard Leary, pastor of Our Lady Queen of Peace. A doctor associated with a clinic that is associated with Catholic Charities and its home for unwed mothers. Maeve waits until Judy is alone in her room, then brings her a card with the name and address, the appointment time, written on it. Maeve tells Judy how to take the bus, and then the T to his office. She hands her transportation money.

"We'll expect you back about 4," she says and leaves.

Judy takes a Trailways bus into the city, and then the T to his office in Jamaica Plain. She gets stuck on the name, Jamaica Plain, Jamaica Plain, repeating it over and over to herself, wondering about its origin and promising herself to look it up when she gets home. When she walks into the office, full of pregnant women, many with other babies, toddlers in tow, and all of them discussing their conditions, happily, excitedly, bringing babies into the world, she thinks she's in the wrong place. In a flash she realizes that she is, of course, in the right place. She, too, is with child. She finds a seat in the corner by the coat rack, which is empty. She takes out her book and tries to read *The Stranger*, but Camus' words don't signify. She waits for the doctor for what seems like forever, surrounded by chattering mothers and their offspring.

Judy, a brainy girl, too smart for her own good, Miss Smarty-Pants, her mother often called her, has, for this particular situation, surrounded herself in ignorance; a cape, a cloak of not knowing that she pulls close. Of course, she's seen her mother pregnant many times. Judy was 13 when her baby sister had been born. So she knows all about the big belly, the weight gain, the exhaustion, the pain of childbirth. She understands the big picture. What she doesn't have, and doesn't know she doesn't have, but doesn't want, and conscientiously avoids gathering, are exact details, how the baby gestates and is born. How the process of a pregnancy proceeds and is monitored. She understands that fucking creates babies but she's not clear about, nor interested in, the specifics. Sperm. Eggs. Zygote. Embryo. These grim details repulse her. It's the same way with her art. She loves drawing the figure, is obsessed with it, one teacher said, but can't bear the scientific names of body parts — labia, vulva, scrotum, foreskin. The words make her skin crawl.

Judy sits among the happy moms and waits, oblivious. She has a Hershey bar in her pocket and breaks off little squares, sneaking them into her mouth, letting them melt so nobody will see her chew. Neither of her parents has ever explained to her the facts of life. Her mother never even told her about menstruation. When she was 12, just in the nick of time, her older sister Josie showed her where they kept the big box of pads and handed her an elastic belt with metal hooks dangling front and back. Judy followed the instructions on the box. Everything else she knew, or thought she knew, all of her information and misinformation had been gathered during whispered conversations with her girlfriends.

"Judith Dougherty?" the nurse calls and Judy starts, forgetting, for a moment, that her parents had made the appointment under this other name, her mother's maiden name. Judy follows the nurse to an examination room where she looks, befuddled and appalled, by the examination table, the stirrups.

"Take off all your clothes, hon, everything, bra, panties," the nurse is saying, handing Judy a cotton wraparound robe. "Put this on, with the opening in front."

Judy hesitates, feeling her cheeks, her ears, begin to burn.

"Your first pelvic?" the nurse asks and when Judy looks at her dumbfounded, she says, "Good lord. Do you know what a pelvic is?"

Judy shakes her head and the nurse explains that the doctor would manually examine her, both externally and also internally, through her vagina. He would use an instrument to open her to make sure that everything inside, the fetus, was progressing normally.

"Now, climb up there and stretch out," the nurse says and Judy obeys, still confused. "Put your feet into the stirrups, like this, see," she says, taking Judy's left foot and placing it into the metal cup. "Now slide your bottom down the table."

Judy ooches her buttocks toward the table's edge, exposing her own genitals in the most horrific way. Judy presses her thighs, her knees, together.

"That's fine for now, hon," says the nurse. "But when he comes in, you'll have to open up."

The doctor is silver haired, pink-cheeked, and not unkind. This is the phrase Judy will later use to describe him to herself: not unkind. Not unkind. "This is your first pelvic?" he asks, repeating, exactly, the nurse's question. Judy nods, unable to speak. "Try to relax. It will make things easier for both of us."

When he starts to work, Judy begins to vibrate, a deep involuntary movement, as though her body were the plucked string of a standup bass. The nurse stands beside her, patting her shoulder.

"It'll be OK, hon," she murmurs.

Judy feels the cold metal of the speculum, the silky touch of the doctor's gloved hand. Against her will, she remembers Bobby, his touch, his smell, and her body twitches, racked with pain. Bobby. Where was he? Where had he gone?

The nurse rubs her shoulder. "It's OK, hon, it really is," she says. "All of us girls go through this."

"When was your last period?" the doctor asks. Judy remains silent, unable to speak. "It's important," she hears him say. "That's how we figure out the gestational age, and if everything is progressing as it should be."

Judy thinks about Confession, about how, when you went into the lightless cubicle, the priest slid back the curtain on the screened panel between you, and you had to tell him how long it had been: ten days, three weeks, two months, a year, since you last confessed your sins.

"It's been two months, no, maybe three," she says, suddenly confused, unable to remember.

"The baby feels bigger than that. Is it possible that you're mistaken? Lots of women are."

"March, March, I think it was," Judy says, her mouth dusty, her cheeks, her ears, enflamed as heating coils.

"Well, that's a little over four months. That seems more realistic. Otherwise, I'd think you're having a huge baby."

The doctor continues probing, poking, but Judy can't think about what he's doing, what he's seeing. "How did it happen?" he asks. "Were you raped?" His voice is muffled by the drape over Judy's thighs. "Were you in love with somebody who left you?"

Judy cannot answer. She can't acknowledge that he's spoken to her, that he is actually asking her how she became pregnant. She pretends she can't hear. She avoids looking at the nurse who is watching her, bemused.

"Well, it doesn't matter, really. The end result is the same. You're having a baby, Judy. You're about to become a mother. Without a husband, a father for the child. My guess, my educated guess, would be around the holidays, the end of December."

What the doctor says should not surprise Judy, but it does, engulfing her. She's about to become a mother. The nurse removes her feet from the stirrups, helps her to sit up. The room is spinning around her. Around the holidays.

"What's your normal weight?"

Judy hears him, but can't answer.

"How much do you usually weigh?" the nurse asks and Judy manages an answer, 120 pounds, humiliated yet again. She sees the doctor's eyebrows leap over his eyeglass frames when he compares 120 to her weight on the chart.

"You're way out of range here, Jude," he says, and she wants to warn him not to use that nickname. That nickname was reserved. "You're only about halfway through your pregnancy and you've already gained more than recommended, thirty-five pounds. That's dangerous, for you and the baby. The last two months are when the greatest gains occur. That's when the baby doubles in size."

Judy tries burrowing deeper into herself, where maybe she won't hear him or have to answer his questions, but she encounters there the baby, her baby, curled up in its wet sac, gestating.

"If you keep going at this rate, you'll gain about 70 pounds during the pregnancy, which is more than 50 percent of your normal body weight. That's just too much. It's unhealthy, dangerous. The less you gain, the easier it is to get back into shape. And for an unmarried woman ... " His voice trails off.

Now he takes her feet, presses his fingertips into the flesh around her ankles. He asks to see her hands, rubs her fingers. "Rings no longer fit?"

"No rings," she whispers. "I don't own any jewelry."

"But see, you're retaining fluid." He shows her a whitish starburst on her ankle left by his fingertips when he presses there. "Excess fluid. Not a good thing."

The doctor gives Judy a due date of Dec. 28; prescriptions for prenatal vitamins and a diuretic. He puts her on a low-salt, low-fat diet, handing her sheets of blue paper that chart the diet. "Protein, skim milk, fruits and vegetables. That's what will get you through, and give you a healthy baby," he says. "Get rid of the chips, donuts, candy. Try six small meals with skim milk. See you next month. And no more weight, you hear me?"

See you next month.

The doctor leaves and Judy gets back into her clothes. She has a future and this doctor, this office would be in it. Her pregnancy would be in it. No matter what she wanted to believe or how she felt about it.

"If the truth hurts too much, tell a lie. Just make sure it's a good one."

The first time Judy, now Dougherty, hears her father say this, the two of them are speeding just ahead of the morning rush hour on Route 1, from the South Shore, to St. Theresa's Home and Foundling Hospital in Jamaica Plain. A silvery mist covers Boston Harbor. Through it Judy glimpses the glistening city skyline.

"Here's the good one," Joe O'Grady says, jabbing the dashboard cigarette lighter with his thumb. She watches his hand as it hovers by the lighter, grabbing the gleaming knob the moment it pops out. She turns away, not actually wanting to hear the good one but knowing she will anyway. "Here's the good one," Joe repeats through a smoky exhalation. "I mean the reason you'll be gone for what, four, five months at least, the explanation. You're going to Florida, to a small town outside of St. Petersburg. You're going to Florida to take care of your ailing great Aunt Lillian, your grandmother's sister, 82, and widowed, who's recovering from a stroke. You'll be living in Florida helping your ailing great aunt Lillian until she dies or recovers. When you get back, with a flat belly, nobody, not even your sisters, will be the wiser."

The truth that hurts too much is this: Judy, now Dougherty, will be holed up just an hour away, on the far side of the city, secreted in a monastic and expensive cell for unwed mothers maintained by an order of nuns called the Gracious Sisters of the Cross, a group of wizened women with names like Aloysius, Joachim, Bonaventure. Holy hags, Joe O'Grady calls them, noting that they run the home in a manner not dissimilar to the operation of Fort Bragg's Disciplinary Barracks. Which is fine with him. You get what you pay for. Up before dawn for Mass and the first of the day's four sets of prayers. Daily disinfecting of all cells, a passionate cleansing no doubt intended to remove the stain of Original Sin. Here Judy will do penance, atoning for her sins, while awaiting the birth of her misbegotten child. Where Judy will prepare to relinquish to an anonymous couple — a happily married but barren Catholic couple —the child she carries. *Blessed be the fruit of thy womb.*

Judy gazes toward the Boston skyline. The voice of WBZ radio's Dick Summer chatters madly. Slime bubbles in her esophagus, threatening eruption, every time the Chevy wagon bounces over a pothole. Judy's predicament is a problem to be solved and Joe O'Grady is solving it. Everything has been arranged. Already arranged. Infertile couples by the dozens are clamoring for the right to healthy white infants of the type Judy would produce. There are waiting lists! And a very complicated screening process, a matching process, before the couple could be chosen. The baby will be absorbed into that family as if through blood rite, a genetic transformation. Why, at this very moment, half a dozen couples were vying — on their knees praying — for the right to Judy's baby.

"And every one of them will do a better job of raising it than you could," he says.

Judy thinks of this particular trip as yet another phase in her journey though she no longer carries her knapsack, her dog-eared copy of *The Prophet*, her fringed shawl woven through with threads of gold. Instead, she carries, packed in the rear seat, a vinyl suitcase in a color called Lipstick Red that Joe had ordered from the Sears & Roebuck catalogue for her sister Caroline's youth group trip to Montreal. In the suitcase, Judy carries a dozen pairs of huge white cotton bloomers, bras, socks, support hose, flannel nighties and maternity dresses — billowy cotton sacks — also ordered by Joe from the Sears & Roebuck catalogue. He has, of course, checked with the nuns, asking them for a list of clothing and personal items Judy will need during her stay.

Later, when it's over, he will give Judy the receipts for all these items and ask her to repay him. Fair's fair, after all. In what Joe considers an act of generosity and kindness, considering, he's also purchased her a portable Singer sewing machine, some fabrics and some patterns, a way for Judy to keep busy during the long weeks at the home. This is a gift. He will not ask her to repay him. The sewing machine and patterns are in the rear seat beside the Lipstick Red suitcase. Among the patterns are pants and dresses for herself; nighties, dresses, buntings for the baby, which if Judy sews them, her father has explained, will be a lovely gift for the misbegotten babe to carry into its adoptive home. As Joe speeds through traffic and a silver mist wafting off the harbor, Judy again glimpses the girl who looked exactly like herself, only thinner, wrapped in a gilded shawl, leaping and pirouetting in a meadow. Beyond the dancing girl she sees, sprawled in the grass, the boy, playing a harmonica. She watches for some time, but cannot hear the music. She feels nothing, not even curiosity. She has no idea, but does not wonder, what happened to the shawl, the knapsack, her copy of *The*

Prophet, the harmonica, the boy. All are artifacts of someone else's life. She herself is a ghost now, insubstantial, drifting through her own afterlife.

"You know this place, this St. Theresa's, is costing me a bundle, a bloody fortune." Judy turns toward her father. "Those nuns, those so-called Gracious Sisters of the Cross, aren't so gracious when it comes to charging for their services."

But St. Theresa's, Joe intones, is an investment in Judy's future, a future that would look bright if only she realized she had to live in the real world. If only she had the wisdom and maturity, the sense of responsibility, to accept it. If only she had enough will power, to put her nose to the grindstone and make up for the time she's lost; to make up for her mistakes. Do her penance and move on.

"If only, if only, you knew how to be good," he tells her, cracking the window on his side so that the cigarette smoke is pulled outside. "You've got some goodness in you, if only you could find it." Of course he, her father, has already forgiven her her sins. How could he not? It was his job, as father, to forgive. And besides, a hand far more powerful than his had meted out rough justice. Rough, indeed. But whose fault was it? Huh? Judy herself was entirely at fault. She herself had made the mess, caused the problem, by choosing the path, the collision course, she'd chosen. She'd flown out of the nest with neither care nor thought — too smart, too good, for all of them. She had nobody to blame but herself.

"Look how far you got before falling flat on your face," he says. "Before coming back to me, on your knees, with your hand out."

"Didn't I warn you? Didn't I tell you those hippies, the so-called peaceniks, flower children, with their drugs and dirty hair, are nothing but a bunch of phonies and users? Living off their parents while destroying everything we worked for. Didn't I warn you? Didn't I tell you? But you wouldn't listen. Are you listening now? Peace and love. Hah! What bullshit. Pardon my French. What bitter irony."

Joe lights another cigarette.

"What can you give this child?" he asks now as if for the first instead of the umpteenth time. "What do you know of mothering? You've already proven yourself to be irresponsible. How do you plan to assume the responsibilities of motherhood? Where will you live? How will you support yourself? Do you know how much diapers cost? Shoes?"

Judy understands his questions are rhetorical. He does not expect answers and she doesn't give them. She tries not to hear his questions, prays silently for deafness, a loss of her own senses.

"You better believe whatever couple wins this particular prize will give him, or her, God knows what it will be, a good home, a great home," Joe is saying. "So much better than you can. It will have two parents, a mother and a father. Both grown-ups, years older than you. With so much more wisdom, maturity. Think of what they'll be able to give it. Private schools. A first rate college. A good name. They'll be able to give this baby a good name. You're just a kid, Jude. What can you give it?"

Judy knows that love isn't the answer, and she won't say it. Love. The word would make her father laugh, snort, breathe smoke, shake his head. Love is cheap, Joe would tell her. Love won't pay the rent. Love won't pay the doctor bills or buy the diapers.

"Don't tell me love, sweetie," he intones as Judy looks out the window. "I'm not interested in love. Love's what got you into this mess in the first place, isn't it?"

No, Judy knows that love is not the answer and she does not

offer it. Instead, she watches the highway and the city racing toward them, and tries to ready herself for whatever's coming next.

Marie and Her Sons

Mayhem every morning: a young mother trying to feed and dress her kids and get them off to school. It started around 7. Up early myself, I'd make coffee, then go sit close to the living room windows of my apartment and watch the drama in the apartment across the airway, as riveting as it was unnerving. A silent movie loaded with action that edged toward danger, danger an audience could sense and enjoy long before the characters on the screen. Three little boys driving their young mother ever closer to the edge. What was the edge? I wondered. We lived on the fourth floor of a five-story walk-up, a long drop to the concrete alley below. No child guards on the windows over there. Maybe that was it.

This happened in the Bronx, back when it was burning. Arson fires everywhere, some set by landlords eager to get rid of loser properties; others by tenants enraged by their miserable housing conditions. (If they got burned out, the city would help them move.) Smoke hung forever in the bedraggled borough's air. Soot peppered windowsills and residents often tasted ash. Ululating sirens were incessant background music.

Valentine Avenue where we lived is narrow, curves like a long bow, running southeast between 204th Street down to Poe Park on the Grand Concourse. That park is a tiny patch of green with a little cottage where the writer and his wife once lived, a place by then littered with discarded syringes and glassines bags where no sane person ventures after dark. Our building, 2674, was one of 10 identical buildings on the block between 194th and 196th streets, dubbed 'the Ten Commandments. Ours was "Honor Thy Father and Thy Mother,' the first building to go empty on that block. The one next door, the focus of my peeping, was 'Thou Shalt Not Kill.'

These buildings, built just after the turn of the century (the 19th, not the 20th), had been gems — oak parquet floors, 10-foot ceilings — built for a nascent middle class, Irish and Jewish. The buildings were smallish, divided by an interior central staircase, five units on each side of the stairs; five rooms in each. Elaborate plaster moldings had once embellished walls and plaster medallions ringed the ceiling fixtures, originally gas light. Big windows on three sides. Southwestern light poured through the ones in the kitchen and living room from just past noon until the sun went down.

My husband and I, refugees from a tiny Lower East Side apartment just outside Chinatown, were unlikely urban homesteaders. We'd been college sweethearts, bonded by our passion for the anti-war movement, but once that war was over, the one between us began. Our marriage was foundering when we met our old college friends at a dive bar on Delancey Street, and they told us about their plan to turn an empty Bronx building into a tenant-owned co-op. At the time, neither of us knew what to do with our lives. We'd moved to New York right after college because I wanted to be an actress, though not a movie star. My husband drove a cab while I tried to make my mark in political theatre. After five intense years of effort, I hadn't gotten anywhere. Well, for a season, I'd been a wardrobe mistress, doing costume repairs for Andre Gregory's Manhattan Project. Much as I loved that man and his productions, I didn't want to be a seamstress. Watching those actors work (Alice Through the Looking Glass) while I fixed their costumes made me sick with longing. I was bruised and confused and ready for a change when we met our old friends for that drink.

Our first trip up to the Bronx, on the D train, excited me. I was looking into the lives of other people, the kind of precarious lives I didn't think I'd ever have to live. The door to what became our apartment hung open on its hinges, and its only occupant was a mangy mongrel. The floors were so filthy the heaps of dog shit almost blended in. The stench. Broken windows. No electricity. No functioning plumbing. I was enchanted.

Our group moved in as squatters. Nobody noticed or cared. It might sound crazy but it was easy back then. By the mid-70s, the city found itself owning, through landlord tax default, many thousands of old apartment buildings, most of them decrepit. It was eager to get such buildings rehabbed or demolished. Months of our killer labor —'sweat equity' — (we didn't outsource anything) followed to make the building livable. We hustled to find government grants for a new boiler, new windows, repairs on the roof, the electrical wiring and plumbing. Among other things, I refinished the oak floors by myself, and scraped through decades of paint until the glass panes of the interior French doors, transoms, and crystal doorknobs gleamed. I particularly loved our ancient Royal Rose gas stove, both the inside and outside gleaming by the time I got through with them. Once the building had been issued a new certificate of occupancy, we bought it back from the city for $2,500 — $250 for each apartment.

The others in our group were the real deal. They included tenant organizers, EMTs in training, public defenders and the Jesuit chaplain at Rikers Island. They were focused on the catastrophic cycle of housing deterioration and landlord abandonment (white flight) that was going on. They'd save the building, then the block, then the world. I was mostly along for the ride, my perspective narrower, focused on my failing marriage, my doubtful future. I'd start grad school in the fall even though I wasn't sure I wanted to be a social worker. Sometimes the others, with their passion and skills and commitment, made me feel vaguely ashamed. I had a lot of trouble sleeping there.

Pulley clotheslines on all five floors were strung from our building to the one next door striping this air space like lines on composition paper. Tube socks, bras, jeans, tighty-whiteys, lacey thongs, sheets and pillowcases hung forever on these lines, flapping wildly when the wind was up, as if a flock of albatross had just alighted on the lines between our buildings.

The clotheslines never stopped my solitary peeping. That apartment across the alleyway didn't have shades or curtains; our big double windows offered a clear view. After dark, with lights on over there, I could see their goings on as if on a big screen, but the morning show was more entertaining.

Those boys, tiny featherweights, bobbed and weaved and feinted, as their mother, their poor young mother, chased them down, caught one, while another escaped. She'd threaten them with whatever weapon she might have close by, a broom, a spatula; most often, just her own two hands. A solid smack upside the head.

Sometimes she'd grasp a flailing arm or leg, and dig her fingers into flesh, but her violence didn't work. The chaos continued until she, one way or another, she got the boys downstairs, and outside, to wait in front of our buildings for the little yellow school buses that picked them up, one by one, to take them off for the day.

I couldn't tell one of those kids from the other, never figured it out, not even after the mom, Marie, and I made friends downstairs on the sidewalk. The boys, dark-haired, light-skinned, were an undifferentiated blur of skinny arms and legs as they squabbled half-dressed, fighting breakfast, fighting clothes, fighting the need to go to school. Red or white sneakers went airborne to unknown destinations along with the occasional Matchbox truck or superhero figure. Bowls of Fruit Loops or Count Chocula (I guessed) and milk flew against the windows, leaving translucent patterns in the morning light.

From my living room, I could almost reach across the air space to touch them. Almost. If, like an angel of mercy, I could fly across that airspace, I'd be able to help her get her kids under control. I'd grown up in a big Catholic family, pressed early into childcare and household service. Ours had been a crazy clean household ruled over by a crazy clean mother. *Cleanliness is next to godliness, blah, blah, blah.* Never believed it; had no desire to become a mother. Even so, I was certain I could help my neighbor get herself and her kids together.

Lay out their clothes the night before, I'd have ordered her, *along with their school bags, with homework and all the other necessary items packed inside.* That way, no frustrating last-minute hunts for a sock or undershirt; for homework. In the morning: *separate them! Lock one in a bedroom if you have to. Focus on one kid at a time; underwear first, shoes last...Hands, face, teeth scrubbed before the final inspection, the rush downstairs for the bus...Never ever try to do all three boys at once.* How could a mother with three little kids be so ignorant of such basic parenting skills?

Sometimes, watching them, fighting a deep unease, I wondered, why am I here? Even though I knew the answer: — I was there to save the building, the block, the borough, and then the world.

The Ten Commandments edged the sidewalk — no setbacks, no stoops. Just two white marble steps up to the glass-paned front doors. The windows of the first floor apartments opened directly onto the sidewalk. But the sidewalks were slate, 12 to 14 feet wide. The buildings and sidewalks were built before anyone foresaw motor vehicles as the premier choice in transportation, even though a D train stop, Kingsbridge Road, was mere steps away. By the time we got there, cars, beaters of all makes, a vehicle in almost every family, lined both sides of the street. City buses, air brakes forever squealing, could barely squeeze through the sclerotic space left between them.

Morning and afternoon, in almost any type of tolerable weather, neighbors appeared outside with their fold-up beach chairs, the kind with metal frames and woven plastic strips. Everybody had one, tucked just inside their front doors. If you wanted to get the scoop about neighborhood goings on, that's where you had to be. Once I'd realized my neighbor brought her boys downstairs every morning to catch their school buses, I, the nosy neighbor, went downstairs, too. Maybe I was thinking that I could give her some parenting advice, or maybe I wasn't thinking at all, just being nosy.

All children are beautiful: one of my most cherished beliefs. I'd heard it said with great conviction countless times: *There's no such thing as an ugly child.* In my family and the families of my friends, big prosperous families, it had been demonstrated countless times: All children are, in their own ways, beautiful. *No ugly children!*

The first time I got to see the neighbor boys up close shattered my conviction. I'd gone downstairs where they waited for their little yellow school buses. Close up, they were sad, raggedy ass children in dirty mismatched clothes with crazy haircuts — whatever, I guessed, their mother managed to chop off when she got hold of them. But that wasn't what stunned me. Up close, their faces seemed blurred, misshapen. With their backpacks, like turtle shells, attached to their backs, they grunted and jabbered, made all kinds of odd noises. I didn't understand the words. At first, I thought they might be speaking a foreign language — Esperanto? Swahili? But then I realized they couldn't talk. They had no language, not a single word, not even Mom or Mama, a fact so shocking I temporarily lost my own. The wild boys across the air space were nonverbal. Not one of them could speak.

The mom's name was Marie, though I hardly remember our hasty introductions. Marie was in her late 20s maybe, hard to say, just a few years older than me. She'd been pretty once. I glimpsed that fresh-faced girl beneath this overwhelmed and ancient woman. A natural strawberry blond, she'd intensified her color into carrot orange. She told me proudly that her boys' names were Charlie, Frankie and Jose. They were nine, eight and seven years old.

The little yellow buses came and rumbled away with one boy after the other. I went back upstairs wondering if they were victims of some biblical scourge, an affliction so frightening that it might, in other times and cultures, have resulted in its victims being shunted off to a gulag, a distant island, somewhere out of sight and touch with other humans. In New York City, in the late 1970s, they were bused to schools, separate schools, for children with special needs.

Outside, Marie was always cheerful, smiling, sweet-faced, and grateful for other grown-ups to talk to. No matter what the weather, she wore dollar store T-shirts, sweatpants bought from sidewalk peddlers, and white canvas sneakers, Keds knock-offs, selling for $3 at the Bargain Bin around the corner. Her teeth, several missing, were edged gray/black; her eyes an exhausted, red-rimmed green. The pudge around her middle was no doubt earned by eating the greasy foods sold by the bodegas and food trucks in our neighborhood. Chorizo. Pork rinds. Fried plantains. But something else was as evident as her boys' affliction: Marie loved them, and tended to them, to the best of her ability. She was devoted to her sons.

I was stunned to learn that Marie was not a single parent. Her husband, Jose, the father of her three boys, lived upstairs in the apartment with them, but he wasn't feeling well. He wasn't ever feeling well. He could no longer go up and down the stairs. So he couldn't help her all that much. Frankie, Charlie and Jose had the same two parents! And they lived in an intact family, something as rare in that time and place as a reindeer trotting down the street.

The boys shared many facial features that had not emerged from any gene pool. These I had to research before I understood them: smooth philtrums, that dented flesh between the nose and upper lip; thin upper lips and small eye openings, aka palpebral fissures. All three had mismatched ears — not just jutting outward, but curiously misshapen, asymmetrical, as if stuck onto their skulls hastily, wherever the ear-maker could find a spot. Fetal alcohol syndrome, I realized with slow, seeping dismay. That's what all three boys suffered from. FAS. Which meant that their facial distortions signaled deeper distortions within, malformations of the central nervous system and the brain, deviations resulting not just in retardation, but in hyperactivity, an inability to concentrate, to learn; poor impulse control.

Faces only a mother could love, I thought, and love them she did, hard as it was for me to imagine. So we stood there many mornings that fall, sunlight in slivers brightening the canyon of Valentine Avenue, Marie and I, and a few other mothers, plus the gathering of old women in their chairs who loved watching the young, not just Marie's brood, but others walking to the nearby Catholic school, Our Lady of Refuge.

Drunks and half-mad glue sniffers also wandered in and around us. Music, salsa, disco, reggae, early hip-hop blared from boom boxes placed in open windows or on the hoods of cars, competing for attention with the sirens. Fetal alcohol syndrome. Three in rapid succession. How could such a thing have happened? She must bear guilt for what she caused. How could she not? But I couldn't ask her much, couldn't poke and prod. Every time I tried, the needles of my middle-class values turned back to prick me. Well, she and Jose, the father, they'd been so in love.

He's the love of my life. He took such good care of us until he got sick.

Somehow or other, with little access to health care system, and no prenatal care, all three boys burst forth before Marie understood she shouldn't drink while she was pregnant.

Day after day, the boys carried on, making their crazy gurgles and wha-wha sounds, which Marie seemed to understand. Outside, we watched them leap and jump around and punch each other while we waited for the buses to take them off to school. Then Marie would smile and sigh and shake her head in relief. Respite for a few hours. She smoked three cigarettes a day, all she could afford. She'd light the first as soon as that last bus departed, inhaling as if an elixir.

We did not become good friends, Marie and I. As the weather cooled, and the work in my grad program intensified, I was less inclined to go downstairs, either in the morning, or later, when the boys came home from school. At some point my peeping ended. I put up drapes on my living room windows, pinch-pleated, bought at Macy's.

Of course, I told Marie that if she ever needed anything to give me a holler. She didn't have a telephone, but every now and then, she'd open her window, and shout across the air space to get my attention. Then I'd make a call or two for her: to one of the kid's schools; to the welfare office; to a doctor. And when one of the men in our building was putting the required child guards on our windows, I asked him to go over and install some on Marie's windows, too. I felt better after her windows had child guards, as if I'd accomplished something that mattered. Once, after the guards were installed, I saw one of the boys gnawing on the windowsill. *Don't let the boys chew the windowsills,* I yelled over to Marie and then repeated it to her downstairs on the sidewalk. *Don't let the boys chew on the windowsills. There's lead paint under there. It poisons the blood, causes brain damage.* She smiled at me, bewildered. *Lead paint causes brain damage,* I repeated.

As the holidays and winter came in, Marie and her boys slipped from my mind and from my heart. My angel of mercy wings shriveled.

In early February, a catastrophic blizzard hit the northeast, one of the worst in the city's history, almost 30 inches. For two days, snow whirled around our buildings, blurring images, muffling sounds. One hundred people died. We lost heat and power for a day, but we were safe and cozy in our building, heaping on blankets, reading by candlelight, sharing meals of lentil soup, Spanish rice, quesadillas.

Once we got to go back outside, mountains of grimy frozen snow made labyrinths of the sidewalks. You couldn't see around corners or even what was up ahead. The cold kept most everyone inside for days at a time. No sooner was the city limping back to normal, when the school bus drivers of Local 1181 of the Amalgamated Transit Union called a wildcat strike, 6,000 of them. In the long painful history of labor strikes in New York City, theirs was a mere blip, recalled by hardly anyone. It occurred in the midst of a rogue wave of labor unrest. Workers' unions as diverse as the corps de ballet at American Ballet Theatre, the city's grave diggers, and bet takers at OTB had walked off their jobs, demanding the usuals: job security, higher wages; better benefits. Milk delivery drivers, umpires at Yankee Stadium, tugboat operators. State prison guards, apartment building service workers. Employees of the New York Historical Society, the Long Island Railroad.

The strikes, according to the New York Times, created pockets of dysfunction in the poor parts of the city. Pockets of dysfunction. Several weeks passed before I noticed the one in the apartment next door, among the deepest and most troubling. I'm pretty sure we sent milk and bread and cereal over for Marie and her kids, but I can't say for sure. But worst of all, those little yellow school buses, the ones that had arrived so promptly every morning, to whisk away Frankie, Charlie, and Jose, no longer showed. No respite for Marie. No routine for her sons. They were trapped at home.

136

Soon after the blizzard, an ambulance pulled up out front, its siren wailing, echoing up and down the block, its red lights splattering our buildings with their awful light. I ran downstairs, thinking it was one of the boys, or, God forbid, Marie herself. I got downstairs just in time to see a man, apparently the mysterious *paterfamilias*, the father of Frankie, Charlie and Jose, stretchered out of the building and into the ambulance. He looked enormous, a bloated sea creature washed up on shore. I don't know how those brawny EMTs got him down the four flights, but they did, then they sirened him away. He didn't return. End stage cirrhosis, I heard.

Soon after, days, not weeks, the third-floor tenants who lived in the apartment under Marie, complained that water was flooding down from the fourth floor. I heard the story afterward, from the med student in our building who rescued her. That morning, Marie had tried bathing her three sons and then herself. She started drinking the water and couldn't stop. Nor did she shut the water off. It kept running and running, cascading over the sides of the deep claw foot tub, and finally through the floor into the apartment below. By the time he got there, Marie was comatose, her face barely above the water. Turned out that she'd drunk so much water that the sodium levels in her blood had plummeted, pushing her close to death. Water intoxication. Extreme hyponatremia. She almost drank herself to death. Then, like her husband before her, Marie was rushed off to Lincoln Hospital and the boys disappeared into the city's child protective services. Neither Marie nor her children ever came back to Valentine Avenue.

Afterward, looking across the air space to the dark apartment with its boarded over windows, I thought about Marie's meltdown, the edge she'd finally found, in her own bathtub. She'd found it bathing her children and herself, bathing as if to cleanse herself of all her sins and failings. Drinking water until she almost burst. A purifying ritual, washing away the impossibilities of her life, an ablution and an absolution.

By the time the strike was finally over, in mid-May, Marie's husband was dead, and she'd lost her three sons to 'the system.' Marie herself, as far as anyone of us could find out, was being treated in a psych ward somewhere in the city. I don't know what became of her or her boys. I never knew her last name. As for her apartment, volunteers from the community repaired and rehabbed it. Once it again became habitable, some missionary nuns moved in.

In the decades since, I've held onto this memory of the red-headed mother and her three damaged boys. Or, rather, I should say, the memory has held onto me, a small piece in the puzzle of my life, a piece I can't force into place. In the years since, through all the changes in my life, and especially since my marriage righted itself and I became a mother, Marie and her sons have haunted me. Diligent, helpless Marie and her three wild, voiceless boys.

I can still see, from the window across the way, their moon-pale faces, staring with bottomless brown eyes, out into the shadows. I've wished her comfort and solace while searching for my own, and think I could have, should have, done more. Back then, I didn't know who I was, and had only the dimmest notion of who I might become. My heart and brain occupied separate territories; a swath of uncertainty roiling in between. A ghostly patrol forever rumbled along this border to prevent any crossing. Still, the scalpel of Marie's story cut me deep and clean, a story that stopped but did not end.

Violets

"YOU GIRLS HAVE IT SO EASY NOWADAYS," Mom told me as she pressed down one of the sticky tabs on my baby's diaper. Violet, my first, just four months old, was lying on her changing table, cooing and flailing her chubby arms and legs, with Mom hunched over her. "These things are a miracle."

My mother, long divorced from Daddy, had Metrolinered down from Boston to help me out for a week or so because my husband was away on business. It was the first time we'd been alone together for as far back as I could remember.

"Maybe for moms." I spoke from my seat in a rocker by the nursery window. "But those miracles don't biodegrade. They're wreaking havoc on the environment." Mom echoed Violet's coos, nuzzled her tummy, then slid her into a pink onesie decorated with tiny sheep. "Nobody's figured out how to dispose of the disposables." Mom didn't answer. Maybe she didn't hear me. Or maybe she wasn't interested in the possible ecological hazards of disposable diapers. She'd never been much interested in the world outside the home.

I considered repeating myself, adding grim details, like how the diapers, distributed free to South Pacific island women, as part of an international marketing strategy, had been washing up along the beaches of Pago Pago. How the soiled diapers, barged out into the ocean and dumped beyond the coral reefs, made their way back on tides and waves, poisoning fish and strangling birds along the way, before they ended up rotting on the beach. The photo in the newspaper showed them, shimmering, gray-white, like dead sea birds, beneath the tropical sun.

Mom laughed softly, rubbing her nose on Violet's. Then, somehow one-handed, she wrapped the used baby wipes inside the soiled diaper and used the tabs to fasten the diaper into a tight ball. She dropped it into the pail, decorated with a pink duck-shaped deodorant, attached to the changing table.

"Only number one," Mom said.

We'd vowed, my husband and I, when deciding to use disposables, that we'd always flush Violet's bowel movements into the toilet before putting the diaper into the trash. I'd passed that instruction on to my mother. Our little effort to save the world.

"You'd never know a baby poops and pees in here," Mom declared then. She inhaled deeply, nodded happily. Then she cooed some more into Violet's face, grasping Violet's pudgy legs and kissing one pink foot, then the other.

"Well, I'm switching to cloth as soon as I can get organized. I'll do a diaper service. Cloth's so much better for the environment."

"Oh, you girls, you have it so easy nowadays," Mom, the queen of repetition, said again. It was a ping or a ding. She smiled, enchanted, at my daughter.

"Easy? What's so easy?"

Mom turned around, holding Violet on her hip, bouncing her a little. She looked around Violet's perfect pink nursery, taking in the crib, the changing table, the toys, the mobiles. *'All the necessary yuppie stuff,'* she'd said when she first saw it. Now she shook her head as though the answer to my question was self-explanatory. "They make everything so easy for you now, but none of you want babies anymore."

She didn't look at me, instead made silly faces at Violet.

"Of course we want babies." I wailed. "We do so want babies. Maybe even more than women in your generation did. But we make an active choice about when to have them, and how many."

"Well, honey, your active choice took just about forever. You almost ran out of time. Why, you're almost 35. In my day, women had all of this behind them at that age."

Mom put Violet back into her crib, then watched her, her hands on her hips, her eyes deep with love. *Had she ever looked at me that way?*

"My birthday isn't for six months."

"Hah!" She chuckled, having proven, she believed, her point.

"Well, 35 is young today."

"You girls think you can control everything."

Mom shook her head, still smiling, at what I couldn't guess. Something jumped inside my belly, as if the baby weren't yet born.

"No, no we don't." My voice pitched higher than I wanted it to. At that moment, I felt I couldn't control anything, and especially not my mother. I began to wish she hadn't come. I knew we'd get into a fight. We always did. "But we can control the sizes of our families. And when we start them. We're not passive victims of our husbands. Or of fate."

I watched her go off, humming, to pick up a basket full of Violet's clean laundry. She began to fold and stack her sleepers and swaddles on the shelves under the dressing table.

"I had three babies in diapers at the same time and that was long before I hit thirty. No disposables back then."

Violet made a fussing sound. Mom picked her up out of the crib and bounced her gently. Violet's head bobbed against her shoulder. I couldn't count all the times I'd heard Mom make this declaration, and she always made it with the same inflections, like a poem she'd memorized. *I had three babies in diapers at the same time...and that was long before I hit 30.* Her great accomplishment. She always said 'hit' instead of 'reached' or 'turned,' — as if the age of thirty were a wall she'd smashed into.

"Seems like, all through my twenties, all I ever did was diapers, washing them by the hour and hanging them on the line." Another of Mom's repeated lamentations.

"But that was good for the environment." I envisioned the diapers on the beach at Pago Pago; knew countless other millions of them moldered in landfills across the United States.

At the newspaper where I work, nobody thought I was too old to be having my first baby. It never once came up. My colleagues and editor thought it made perfect sense for me to wait until I had some seniority, a good salary, and could pick and choose my hours, before I began my family.

"Why you'll be forty-something at the first grade Christmas party," Mom said.

"Heaven forbid!"

Mom laughed in a way that made me want to strangle her. Now I was really sorry that she'd come. She always made me doubt myself.

"And think of high school graduation! You'll be in your fifties, menopausal. As for college, well, we won't even go there."

"Menopause is just mid-life, now," I said. She gave me a look, like maybe I suffered from post-partum dementia.

My medical chart at the hospital had described me as an 'elderly primapara.' I asked the nurse what on earth that meant, and she told me: an old first-time mother, old being anyone over 30. *What a goof, me, an elderly primapara.* How Matt and I had laughed, but I won't tell Mom. More fuel for her fire.

My mother's a short, small-boned woman whose once-tiny waist was now encircled by cummerbunds of flesh. Her arms and legs were still as thin as always. Lately she'd been laughing at her own shape. Mrs. Potato-Head, she called herself, making the joke before anybody else could, a habit she'd always had, and repeating it at every chance. Back to the laundry, she worked slowly, caressing each little undershirt, nightgown and stretch suit before she put it on a shelf. Once I caught her holding something to her face, sniffing to inhale the baby's amazing smell, just the way I did. She was humming My Blue Heaven.

Still I was unsettled. With my mother I always felt an awful friction, the grinding between tectonic plates. Usually Matt or one of my sisters was around to smooth the roughest edges. Not now. But my mother had insisted upon coming, would have even if I hadn't invited her. *The birth of your first child is...Well, I'd given up hope. I thought I'd never see the day...*

We met her at the train station in Philadelphia and drove home to our house in the 'burbs. She cried when she first laid eyes on Violet. I'd felt a ping then, too. *Had my mother wept with joy for me?*

My hands rested on the soft, empty sack of my stomach. I was afraid it would never tighten up again. Mom lingered over the laundry. I wondered if the mysterious eternal conflict between us might be one reason I waited to have children. I wanted to be sure I was mature enough to do a better job than she had done.

"You must remember the cloth diapers," Mom said as if from a great distance. She spoke softly, happily, oblivious to my anger. "It wasn't so long ago. All that wash. Then hanging them out by hand."

My mother had been one of six girls, and she'd had six girls herself. And I did remember her, at the backyard clothesline, placed low into the ground so she could reach it, her head and upper arms hidden by the flapping white wings all around her.

I'd grown up near the water, on the Fore River, not far from Quincy Bay. Summer squalls could blow in almost without warning. Mom was forever rushing outside to haul in diapers just before the downpour. I watched her from a kitchen window, worried because she looked so small; afraid she might be carried off, up into those storm clouds, by the ferocious flapping birds she was trying so hard to capture.

"The worst part was the dirty diapers always soaking in the toilet, and then, into the bucket next to it." Mom, finished with the laundry, walked back to the crib. Yes, I remembered that stench, a sharp ammonia smell. On her tiptoes, Mom reached over to wind up the Sesame Street mobile attached to its far side. "You couldn't get away from the stink," she said. "Dan Doyle hated it so much!"

"Dan Doyle?"

"Your father," she said, as if I didn't know.

"Of course I know he's my father. I just don't get why you call him that. Dan Doyle. Like he's somebody we hardly know."

"Do I?" she asked. "Is that what I call him?"

"Either that, or Daddy. Like he's your father, not your ex-husband.

Mom shrugged, mystified. "Dan Doyle, Daddy, whatever. I don't know what else I should call him."

"Well, I don't either. But one's too distant, and the other's too close. Incestuous, or something."

"Oh, please!" Mom straightened up, then flicked Big Bird and Cookie Monster so they spinned and danced. Violet cooed and tried to lift her head. The mobile played Twinkle Twinkle Little Star.

"Oh, look!" I got up to see. Mom pointed to Violet's dimpled grin. "Looks like she's in heaven." My mother's name was Virginia, which she, for some reason hated. Daddy always called her Ginny or just Gin. She'd made all of us promise we'd never use that name for our daughters. Not that any of us would have.

Mom reached through the crib rails to touch my daughter's cheek. Her fingers were bent from rheumatoid arthritis, an ailment she contracted in her 20s. The way her fingers curled, she always looked like she was grasping for something, or trying to hold on.

"It doesn't mean anything," I said as Violet's smile disappeared. "They're called angel smiles. It's a reflex." Mom turned to look at me, her green eyes full of pity. "It says so in one of my books. The facial muscles aren't yet connected to any emotions."

Now it was early evening and we sat close to a crackling fire because my living room turned chilly when the sun went down. Mom and I, both of us former Girl Scouts, had struggled with the fire, arguing about how to get it going. She finally succeeded using some of the hickory kindling I'd given Matt for Christmas. Mom and I were drinking dark imported beer. Matt brought home a case after he'd read that one of its ingredients helped lactating mothers produce milk. Mom drained her glass, refilled it from her bottle on the coffee table.

"God knows I'm not lactating," she said, "but I can still enjoy this."

I held Violet, warm and drowsy, against my chest. When I stroked her cheek, she turned toward my finger, her bud mouth opening and closing. This, too, was a reflex she'd eventually outgrow. She was rooting for my nipple, searching for her food source. The instinctive movement helped insure her survival. Blew me away every time she did it. Mom had fed all of us baby formula. *Had we kids rooted for the baby bottles?* I wondered but didn't ask.

I touched Violet's cheek with my nipple and she clamped her mouth over it. My breast filled up, milk tingling through its ducts. Violet made a tiny humming sound every time she swallowed. Mom watched us intently, her gaze scraping me just a little.

"How do you know she's getting enough?"

"She takes what she wants and that's enough." I knew my mother would question my breastfeeding, so I'd prepared an answer— with help from *The Womanly Art of Breastfeeding*. "It's the perfect example of supply and demand. Your body supplies exactly what the baby demands, and the baby demands exactly what she needs. No fuss, no muss, no waste, no cleanup."

"I don't think anybody ever asked me if I wanted to," Mom said. A moment passed before I realized she meant breastfeeding. "No, nobody ever did. It just wasn't done back then. In the hospital, no questions asked, they gave you a shot to dry up your milk the minute you delivered. Everyone said it wrecked your figure, that formula was better." She shrugged. "Dan Doyle would've been embarrassed if I tried."

"Violet was doing this not 15 minutes after she was born." Maybe I was bragging, just a little. "They put her right on top of me, as soon as she came out, because they say it's the best thing for bonding. She latched right on and went to town, sucking, like she'd been doing it for years."

"Well, we didn't have bonding back when you kids were born."

"You mean you didn't have the word bonding." I hated when she conflated a word with its experience.

"Is that what I mean?" Mom turned away and looked into the fire. She began to rub her hands together.

"It's an important distinction," I heard myself say, but then hoped she didn't hear me. I tried hard not to let her verbal inexactitude bother me. Still, I couldn't help being a copy editor, or, as Mom liked to say, a smarty-pants, a nitpicker.

Each of my sisters and I harbored some pet peeve about our mother. My oldest sister hated her clothes, a seemingly endless supply of dark polyester pull-on pants and printed over blouses. We joked that she purchased them in bulk from Costco. Another sister, and maybe me, too, hated her hairdo, the kind of short, curly perm that went out of style many years ago. When I suggested to Mom that it was time to try something more up-to-date, she said, 'I love my wash and wear hair. I could care less about how it looks.'

Not long ago, I asked her why she'd stopped wearing lipstick and blush. I'd never seen her without them growing up. She'd always been so careful about her appearance that I thought she slept in make-up. 'Oh, I'm beyond all that now, honey,' she answered. 'And believe me, it's a great relief.'

Despite the successes of her daughters—we've all earned at least B.A.s, and several of us have gone on — my baby sister would soon be awarded her PhD. — Mom considered herself 'down-to-earth.' Oblivious to political correctness, she called us her doctors, lawyers and Indian chiefs. It was hard to tell if she was bragging or complaining.

Once my sisters and I had pooled our money and given her four place settings of Lenox bone china for her birthday, a gorgeous, gold-filigreed pattern I coveted. 'This must be what you want,' she exclaimed, as she opened it, turning to the sister who'd chosen it. Of course it was. We were too embarrassed to even look at one another. We returned the Lenox and bought her plain white Corelle. Mom still raved about those dishes — dishwasher safe, ovenproof, microwave-proof, close to unbreakable — *and they always look so nice. You can see what you're eating!*

Mom was the least pretentious person I knew. At times her lack of pretension felt like a grain of sand stuck under my contact lenses. Again she rubbed her fingers.

"Do they hurt?" I asked. "I've got some ibuprofen."

She shrugged. "Work is good because it keeps them moving. My doctor tells me that's what you've got to do, keep them moving or they'll — what's that word? Ay-trophy? You know, stiffen up for good."

"Atrophy," I corrected. She ignored me.

"Use it or lose it. That's what they joke about at work. But they're not talking about fingers."

After her divorce, my mother got a job at a postal sorting facility on Dorchester Avenue in Boston, a job requiring alertness, manual dexterity, and the ability to multi-task, skills Mom had no doubt developed raising all us kids. She loved her job and what I thought was her meager paycheck. She had no plans to ever retire. *They'll have to carry me out of there in a box,* she'd said more than once, and cackled at the thought of it. Now she sat back and sipped her beer. I moved Violet to my other breast. We listened to the crackling fire.

I was, to my own embarrassment, a failure at natural childbirth. Months later, this failure still rankled, almost as excruciating as the labor. Matt and I went through weeks of conscientious preparation — Lamaze classes, reading endless preparatory texts, eating and exercising exactly as the doulas and midwives advised. Everything we thought we were ready for collapsed against a 14-hour onslaught of contractions. In the labor room, Matt coached me patiently. He held my hand, and huffed and puffed along with me. When my mouth was dry, he found ice chips for me to suck on and when my feet felt colder than the ice, he found wool socks and put them on me. He tracked my contractions on the fetal monitor so he could tell me each time a contraction peaked. 'It's just about over,' he would say and rub my belly as it softened.

Still I felt helpless and alone. I was aware, every moment of every hour, that he didn't feel any pain. The pain was mine alone— and all the preparation in the world couldn't stop it or control it. At the suggestion of our Lamaze instructor, we'd brought along, a tote bag containing many potentially useful items, like the socks, and tennis balls for massages during back labor, and sour flavored lollipops for in case the huffing and puffing dried out my mouth.

Among these items was a paper titled 'What To Do If She Panics in Transition,' the most intense part of labor, just before the baby's head appears, the time women are mostly likely to lose their wits from pain. The paper suggested ways the labor coach could help the woman out of panic, like holding her face hard between both hands and forcing her to focus on his eyes. Or calling her name loudly and slowly, as if to bring her back from someplace far away.

But when I panicked in transition, announcing at the top of my lungs that I was going home, Matt panicked too. He could neither find the instructions, nor recall what they'd said.

I have a clear vision of my husband, just before I got up to leave: rifling through the tote bag, throwing socks and balls and lollipops into the air as he hunted for 'What To Do If She Panics in Transition.' I was repeating my pledge to stab Matt in the heart with the ginsu knife he'd ordered from TV if he ever laid another finger on me when my doctor appeared and ordered me to pull myself together and climb into the birthing chair.

I pleaded for medication, moaning and panting like a beast. 'Too late,' he said, pointing to the chair. Putting on his gloves, he reminded me, that we were in a natural birthing room. 'And you requested it and were trained for it, or you wouldn't be here,' he said. I was so astounded, I came back to myself. I couldn't make another sound. But I could not tell my mother this. I could not tell her how scared I was, or how much it hurt.

"Violet's birth was the most beautiful experience of my life," I told Mom instead, rubbing Violet's back, looking into the fire. *The birthing room was fabulous, so comfortable. The delivery went like clockwork because we were so well prepared. I used psychoprophylaxis to control the pain. Blah blah blah.*

"Psychopropy-what?" Mom grinned, ready for the punch line.

"Psychoprophylaxis. Mental exercises instead of drugs."

She shrugged. I went on: *Matt was a prince. He was with me every minute. I couldn't have done it without him. Birthing Violet together was the pinnacle of our marriage. So far.*

Mom drained her glass. She got up and went into the kitchen. I heard her rummaging through the fridge, then running water, maybe washing a dish or two.

"I don't remember when I first saw you," she called and it occurred to me that she'd never told me my birthing story. She never talked about any of our births. "I get the births of all you kids mixed up," she said above the running water. "Like I was having the same baby over and over again."

"Well, Mom," I called back to her, "I'm the kid who was born in northern Vermont, up near Montpelier. The only one. Does that refresh your memory?"

A few minutes passed. The refrigerator opened and closed again. "You were the one they tried to hold inside me," she said at last. "They held you back because the doctor wasn't there."

Held back! The words rippled through me, and, it seemed, spun backward through my life so far. *Held back!* Mom returned with a tray. On it were two more bottles of beer, a plate of sliced cheese and sliced apples. Her cheeks were flushed.

"The hospital was actually an old mansion, way off in the woods somewhere. You were ready to be born by the time Daddy and I got there. I knew that much because I'd already had two kids."

She sat back down, poured more beer into our glasses. "But the doctor wasn't there yet. So two nurses, big brawny girls, strapped me to a table, then pushed my legs together, and held them, so you wouldn't arrive before the doctor did."

"They could have killed me." I am outraged for myself.

"I was afraid they had."

Mom sat on the edge of the couch, looking into the fire, not at me. Her fingers danced on the glass top of the coffee table.

"You couldn't ever describe that kind of pain. I passed out a couple of times. I was almost 26, but looking back it seems like I was just a kid." My mother swirled the beer in her glass, gazed into it. "Daddy wasn't there, of course. They didn't let the men in back then. I was alone. At first I was afraid to say anything. To tell them to let you come out. Then I was screaming that they had to stop. That's when they covered my mouth and nose with a black rubber mask. Ether. Knocked me out."

Watching her, I realized that she'd probably remembered everything about my birth, about all of our births. She remembered everything that had ever happened to every one of us. But for reasons I didn't understand, she'd tucked these stories away inside herself, mysteries we could not unravel.

"The next thing I remember, I came to, everything was quiet and my belly was flat. I put my hands on it, it was empty but I didn't have a baby. Where was my baby? I was in a huge open ward with carving around the ceiling and a big dusty chandelier. It was full of sick old people, and a lot of them were groaning. I was burning up with a fever. The windows were so high all I could see out of them was gray sky. The ceiling and the sky seemed to be spinning around.

"I was so sick from all the medications I hardly cared if I lived or died. Later I found out that they really damaged me inside by what they did. But the worst thing was I thought you were dead and was too afraid to ask. Nobody paid any attention to me. I thought they were afraid to tell me what had happened. Daddy had gone home by then to take care of your sisters. All night long I lay awake and watched the moon move across the sky, thinking I had lost a baby. It was the longest night of my life."

Mom paused for a swallow of beer, which seemed to take forever.

"The next day Daddy was allowed in for a visit. He looked gray, too, and that scared me even more. But he said we had a pretty daughter. You were out in the hallway in a portable bassinette because they didn't have a nursery. He said you were getting plenty of attention out there because all the nurses thought you were so cute. I was running a fever, Daddy said, and that's why they couldn't bring you to me. They wouldn't let me hold you or feed you. I think they propped the bottle. But then Daddy argued with them, and he brought you in so I could get a peek. I only saw your head, poking out of the swaddling. And then he carried you away again. I don't believe I got to feed you for a week after you were born."

My nipple slipped out of Violet's mouth with a wet pop. She'd fallen asleep. A minute or two passed before I realized Mom had finished her story. Violet snored on my shoulder, a faint vibration. Both of us were drenched in sweat.

Mom got up to put another log onto the fire. She opened the screen, crouched to toss it in and stabbed the fire with a poker. Orange sparks showered her in a hot glow. In this scattering light I glimpsed how the emptiness, or indifference, or whatever it was, between us might have begun, at my birth. No bonding back then.

"You named your baby for my favorite flower," she said then, not looking at me, her statement like a needle into my heart. We hadn't done any such thing. We picked the name only because we liked it. "How I loved those little flowers, so fragile and so tough.

Still do." I'd forgotten all about Mom's love of violets. The memory hadn't surfaced even once when we were thinking about names. "It was such a lovely surprise, her name, Violet."

Visions of Mom's violets filled my mind's eye, tiny flowers growing in wild abundance all around the house, beds of them here and there. Mom encouraged them so they flourished and spread. She could never have too many. When they were in bloom, she put cups and glasses full of them in every room.

Mom came back and sat beside me on the couch, her face flushed with a rare but familiar smile, a look of pleasure or satisfaction like the one she'd gotten tending to her flowers. She'd never gotten it tending to her kids. She reached out to stroke Violet's downy head, and then leaned down to kiss it. She believed our baby's name was an homage to herself, evidence of a special connection between herself and our baby. She'd spread that news to everyone — I knew she would — and especially to Dan Doyle and my sisters. *They named their first baby after my favorite flower!* How could I tell her she was wrong?

I woke up startled, confused for a moment about where I was. Red numerals on the clock beside my bed said it was 4:17 a.m., the longest stretch of sleep I'd had since Violet's birth. I lay there for a moment, torn between the sweet luxury of the long sleep and worry that Violet had missed a feeding. My breasts hurt. I rushed into the nursery, afraid because she hadn't woken up.

The wedge of moonlight that fell across her crib showed that it was empty. My heart threatened to explode before I saw the silhouette in the rocker by the window: Violet in my mother's arms, sleeping peacefully. The chair creaked back and forth.

"I couldn't enjoy my babies when I had them," Mom said so softly I had to strain to hear. "There were too many of you, all at the same time." She kept on rocking, slowly and steadily. I moved closer, thinking she'd offer me my baby. When she didn't, I thought of grabbing Violet from her, asking Mom to leave. "I was like the old woman in the shoe. I didn't know what to do."

Then I felt myself shrinking. I felt how small I was, how small my mind and heart. I stood there shrinking until I was small enough to climb onto my mother's lap. But I didn't. My baby girl, Violet, was already there. Then suddenly, the desire enfolding me like a swaddle, I wanted Mom to enjoy my baby.

I went into the kitchen, where I had a formula gift pack from the hospital, and a breast pump. I fixed a bottle with a nipple and brought it to my mother. She took it and put the nipple into Violet's mouth with a practiced hand. Mom held Violet close. The rocker creaked. In a moment, Violet was sucking as lustily as if she were at the breast. After that I got the pump and figured out how to use it, such a crazy contraption I couldn't help but smile once it got going. Mom and Violet were in earshot — I heard the two of them cooing and sighing — and I saw them in my mind's eye, shadowed in the moonlight: helpless Violet cuddled in my mother's arms, somehow closing the gap between my mother and me, that yawning gap between what each of us had needed and what each of us had gotten. Matt and I had named her Violet — unknowingly — for my mother's favorite flower, sweet and wild and tough and fragile. Again the rocker creaked, the sound of the gap between us inching slowly closed.

WITNESS

MY SHOPPING LIST WAS SHORT: yams and pearl onions for the next day's Thanksgiving dinner; napkins and candles; wine. My baby Lila, nine months old, had been fussy all morning as I baby-sat for several other children in our building on Valentine Avenue in the Bronx, a place we'd homesteaded with a group of friends a couple of years before. The fresh air, I figured, and stroller ride up to 197th Street, would settle Lila down, get her ready for a nap.

The day was sunlit, extraordinarily bright as it poured through the huge south-facing windows of my kitchen, but when we got downstairs, cold wind sucked away my breath. I'd overdressed Lila, the way new mothers often do, in a sweatsuit, a sweater, a hooded jacket. I'd tucked a blanket all around her, but was, myself, wearing just a hoodie, bright pink. On the slate sidewalk, I stood shivering for a moment. I debated whether to go back upstairs for something warmer. If I did, I'd have to schlep Lila, and the stroller, back up all four flights and down again. No way. The produce store wasn't far; the fresh air would do me good.

Valentine Avenue arcs through the central Bronx, more or less parallel to the Grand Concourse, from E. 176th Street up to 201st, a neighborhood long troubled by white flight and arson fires. Our building was atypical, one of ten identical attached five-story tenements, in a neighborhood of big, double-winged buildings. These other buildings, in a style characteristic of the Bronx, enclosed elaborate central courtyards — gargoyled tiers of concrete, forever shadowed by the massive buildings hunched around them. By comparison, our building was minimalist, unadorned. Its first-floor front windows opened directly onto Valentine. Since the turn of the century, when they'd been built, the buildings had dubbed 'the ten Commandments.

I walked north along Valentine Avenue, pushing Lila in her Maxi-Taxi, familiar with every crack and upheaval in the wide slate slabs of sidewalk. We headed to the Korean produce store and a bodega three blocks away, an area as familiar to me as my own face. Walking into the wind, I thought about my mother driving down from Boston to spend the holiday weekend with us. I hoped the corner liquor store stocked a wine other than Night Train. Not that we were fussy. Something pink would do. Blush.

Then I heard a loud bang, loud enough to make me and my baby quake. Then another. Firecrackers, I thought. Wrong holiday. After two they stopped. Some celebration.

I'd already turned toward the sound, to my right, into one of those elaborate but now crumbling courtyards. A man was falling backward, his skull seemingly in two pieces, a spray of blood, bright red, arcing upward as he fell. Another stood beside him, his back to us. One man falling, another watching him fall. The falling man landed, sprawled face up in the courtyard, his arms flung outward, a hasty crucifixion. The standing man looked down, his back to us. Then he was shoving his hands into the pockets of his jacket. His hands. One of them held a gun.

Eons passed. Just ahead of us a little boy, maybe six, was riding a Smurf Big Wheel. He stopped at the sound of the gunshot, leaped off the Big Wheel and rushed toward us. He rushed in slow motion, his arms outstretched. In windows above and all around us, I noticed other watchers, drawn by the sound or maybe already window gazing the outer borough way, leaning on pillows on the sills of open windows.

The shooter stood in plain sight, a few steps beyond my arm's reach, not yet knowing we were there. He was about to turn around; he would have to turn toward us. I knew this as I stood there. Knew exactly what the shooter would do next. He'd turn around and see us. He'd realize we were there, that we'd borne witness. A queer aura, shimmering but transparent, surrounded him, and I watched him transfixed, as though all of us had fallen out of time.

No place to run. No place to hide. No, we had no place to hide. I knew this as surely as I knew that the shooter was about to turn toward us. We, my baby and I, we were trapped, exposed there, on a vast plain of sidewalk, sunlight shining all around us, beautifully, improbably, in that gray canyon of tenements.

I looked down at Lila, my baby, bundled in her fuzzy hooded jacket and sweatsuit, shrink-wrapped in her soft pink blanket. I saw her, my innocent, from that particular perspective, mother pushing stroller. She was leaning forward, holding onto the stroller's handlebar with its bright attachments — rattles shaped like keys, a steering wheel that honked. Lila had two sharp bottom teeth and a third was pushing through. All morning, she'd been squalling.

When I'd tried to rub her gums with Orajel, she chomped down on my finger. She refused to take a nap. Now I willed her not to cry, not to honk her horn. Maybe I touched her head, or murmured something to her. Don't cry, baby, don't make a peep. Then another command, a lamentation, roiled up from somewhere inside me:

Pretend this is not happening, Pretend you are not here. Show no reaction, none at all.

I obeyed. I pretended I could not see the body sprawled, twitching, a few yards to my right, blood splattered on the concrete wall behind it, puddling around the skull. Pretended I could not see the little boy running toward us in slo-mo, his arms outstretched, the Smurf's blue face grinning behind him. Pretended I could not see the shooter, dressed all in black, coming toward us, hunched forward, his hands in the pockets of his zippered jacket, moving quickly, not quite running, but moving fast, focused, intent upon a course that would take him maybe two steps to my right.

The wild voice offered a final urgent command: *Do not look at the gunman. Do not make eye contact. Pretend he doesn't have a face. Pretend you don't either. If you don't look at the killer's face, he won't look at yours — and therefore you will not exist for each other. And not existing for him is the one way you can save your baby and yourself.*

Against my Catholic upbringing, not just the 10 Commandments, but also the beatitudes, the corporal and spiritual works of mercy, the entire Baltimore Catechism, not to mention my own personal convictions, my sense of right and wrong: *Pretend this isn't happening. Pretend everything is fine. Yes, it's all good. Yada yada.* Which is what I did. And thus the killer passed us, so close we almost touched. He passed us, a shadow, and then he disappeared.

This was a flashbulb moment, one so harsh, so bright, it scorched a small place in my brain. Years later, Lila safely grown, I can get back there in an instant, to that late November afternoon, on that slate sidewalk, a new mother with her baby, heading to the store. The two loud bangs, the victim falling, the shooter pocketing the gun — all browns and grays but for the red blood arcing upward. I can feel, even now, how painful it was to resist the urge to run, to scream. How painful to push Lila's stroller forward at the exact pace I'd been going — no faster and no slower. How painful to pretend a little boy in a brown jacket wasn't running toward me with his arms outstretched, his Big Wheel abandoned. To pretend a young man wasn't dying or dead already, just steps away.

The killer walked right past us, heading, most likely to the nearby Kingsbridge Road station on the "D" train. I kept walking, too, pushing Lila in her stroller, floating out of time. A bubble seemed to surround us. At the next corner, I saw a pay phone, dropped in a coin, dialed 911.

"I've just witnessed a murder," I said. "Valentine Avenue and 197th Street."

"How do you know it was a murder?" the dispatcher asked. Her question burst the bubble, and released a vision: the shooter turning around, coming back, opening fire upon us as I stood talking on the phone. I hung up, seized by a violent palsy. I stumbled into the produce store and asked to use their phone. Seeing I'd been somehow traumatized, they fussed over Lila, produced a wooden crate of lettuce for me to sit on, offered me smelling salts. I held Lila on my lap, called my neighbor to come get us. By the time she arrived, sirens were howling all around us, echoing the mad voice in my head. That block of Valentine was a crime scene.

In the aftermath, the story loses clarity. Back in my apartment, while the sirens wailed outside, friends gathered to console me. Four years before, we'd purchased our abandoned building from the city. We'd rehabbed it through sweat equity and a variety of state and federal programs, an experience that forged intimate, familial relationships among us. Many were housing and community organizers. All were veterans of the anti-war movement, passionate street-smart pacifists. Their interest quickly focused not on what had happened, but on my reaction to it. I'd left that guy to die on the sidewalk? I hadn't helped the kid on the Big Wheel? I didn't try to stop the killer?

I couldn't explain my reactions and I soon stopped trying. Just an hour or so later, I started thinking, maybe, just maybe, I hadn't seen what I thought I'd seen, cold-blooded murder on the sidewalk in broad daylight, words from a crime drama on TV. But then the NYPD called. I must have given them my number during the 911 call, though I didn't remember. The victim, they told me, had died instantly of a single shot to the head at point blank range. The second shot was redundant. He was 24, just discharged from the Navy. A drug deal gone bad, a detective said. I hung up, sat alone in the rocker in my darkened living room, nursing Lila, who soon fell asleep.

But I couldn't sleep, couldn't stop that bloody footage from replaying every time I closed my eyes. When I opened them, I kept thinking about Thanksgiving dinner, my mother driving in from Boston, and I still didn't have yams, pearl onions, napkins, candles or wine. A little after 1 a.m., our buzzer sounded, jolting me upright. The NYPD. Two detectives trudged up the four flights to ask if I'd look at a line-up. Two detectives, a tag team sent by Central Casting: middle-aged, one was tall with acne scars; the other stout, with a shaved head. Both looked tough as Doc Marten soles despite their ties and jackets. Service revolvers bulged in shoulder holsters, a threat or promise. How could I say no?

We headed in an unmarked town car to the 48th Precinct, Shaved Head driving, running every red light. They were grateful, really grateful, they kept saying, that I'd called about the murder, and agreed to be a witness.

"Almost never happens around here," Tall One said.

"I'm the only one?" I kept seeing all those other faces in those windows, silent witnesses. Yeah, they assured me. The one and only.

The murder was the result of "a couple of scum bags double-crossing each other," Shaved Head said. The victim had been selling drugs out of that apartment. "No great loss to humanity." His partner nodded agreement.

At the precinct, the first time I'd ever entered one, they sat me in a hard metal chair in a big fluorescent-lit room with peeling gray paint, many bedraggled metal desks. Just like on TV. They brought me a cold Coke. I waited and waited for the assistant district attorney to show up. I showed the detectives on a map where we'd been walking in relationship to where the shooting had occurred. Left mostly alone, I watched indecipherable comings and goings, and had plenty of time to ponder the ramifications of being a witness to murder. Was I ready for it? I kept wondering. Could I handle it? I didn't think so, not without medication. After all, the detectives believed they had their shooter. Already. He was right there in the building with us. And I'd have to identify him, the man I'd pretended not to see. For, although I never made eye contact, and pretended as I passed him that he did not have a face, his face, its planes and angles, its distinguishing characteristics, had taken up permanent residence in my memory bank, bright and immutable. I'd know him anywhere. I figured he could say the same for me.

Time slowed as I sat there. I didn't wear a watch and couldn't see a clock. I was stuck inside a very slow moving dream, hardly any momentum at all. And when, at last, the A.D.A. showed up, sometime between 3 and 4 a.m., he decided the line-up would be "too prejudicial." I didn't hear him say this. Never saw him. I got the news from the furious detectives who explained to me, sarcastically, not believing a word of it, that the 'look-alikes' didn't look anything like the perp they had in custody. 'Bullshit,' said Tall One. 'Fucking bullshit, excuse my French.'

Back we went to the unmarked town car for the return trip to Valentine, Shaved Head again driving, again running all the lights. They apologized extravagantly, and kept repeating the phrase, 'too prejudicial,' a punch line curdled with disgust and anger. Too prejudicial. Despite their hard work, they complained back and forth, a routine they seemed to have rehearsed many times, their lines spoken perfectly, the case "had no priority." It would never come to trial. Such a low priority, it would be pleaded out. The victim, after all, was no great loss to humanity. Blah blah blah.

"He didn't look like a killer," I interrupted their routine, cracking them up. I didn't get the joke.

"What does a killer look like?" Shaved Head asked, laughing again, even louder. "Anyway, you're lucky. Your tickets weren't punched today."

"Tickets?"

"You know, you dodged a bullet. You and your kid."

"Literally and figuratively," said Tall One. "Guy could've just as easily turned the gun on you and your baby. Thank your lucky stars."

That's the thought they left me with as they pulled up in front of our building. I got out. They watched me let myself in and sped off, back to the 48th. By then, the stars were gone. The sky was streaked with pink and yellow light. It was already Thanksgiving Day.

That was it, the end of it. I never again heard from the NYPD. No arrest was ever made. The case never made its way through the Bronx County criminal justice system. Not a word about it was ever reported in the New York City newspapers. Somebody got away with murder. Some people's lives don't matter. Evil exists. In the aftermath of the killing, those thoughts made their way through my life, my heart and mind, leaving an unhealed contusion. For I've never escaped the knowledge of my own raw fear. That I've carried with me, and it is with me still, there, in that scorched place where the calm, efficient murderer abides.

Sifting through my memories, I recall how Lila used to bob up and down in her stroller, kicking the footrest with her heels, and honking the horn on her play steering wheel. How she hummed and gurgled, taking in the world with her big brown eyes. I recall how, those first months of her life, we walked, with our friends and neighbors and their babies, for hours around the Bronx: to Poe Park, over to Mosholu Parkway, around Montefiore Hospital, through the Botanical Gardens, the Zoo, Fordham's Rose Hill campus. We'd scoped out every swing and slide, every corner playground. We were happy homesteaders, living lives of voluntary poverty, intent upon saving, if not the world, then at least our little corner of the Bronx.

That particular Wednesday before Thanksgiving everybody else was busy, so Lila and I went out alone. It was extraordinarily bright with a wind so brisk it sucked away my breath. I'd overdressed Lila, swaddled her in a pink blanket in her stroller, but was, myself, wearing just a sweatshirt. I shivered, but decided against going back upstairs for a jacket. Instead, thinking about yams and pearl onions, and about my mother's visit for the weekend, I pushed Lila forward, north along Valentine Avenue, into the brisk November wind.

So Much Water

WE'D SUNNED OURSELVES ALL MORNING, Mom and I, side by side, on lounge chairs by the swimming pool of my rented vacation condo. Slick with tanning gel, broiling under the July sun, just steps from the Atlantic, we watched my children, Sam and Veronica, cannonball one another, bob under and then explode from the water, liquid crystals spraying high above them. One screeched, "Marco," and the other "Polo." Marco Polo Marco Polo Marco Polo.

"I don't get that game," said Mom, gazing at them from behind her big, black sunglasses.

"It's like tag, or blind man's bluff, but underwater," I said. "They shut their eyes instead of using a blindfold."

"Easy to cheat. Just open your eyes."

"Hard to play with only two."

Again, both kids dove underwater and then exploded out of it, shouting the first, then last, name of the Italian merchant traveler. Marco Polo.

I shrugged. "It wears them out."

"That's a good thing," Mom said, sounding doubtful. She went back to her book, LaVyrle Spencer's *The Fulfillment*, leaving me to keep an eye, both eyes, on my kids, who hardly ever ran out of energy. My book, Garcia Marquez's *Love in the Time of Cholera*, lay unopened on the lounge chair next to me.

The condos, two towers, faced the ocean, and offered water views from our sixth-floor unit. The swimming pool was wedged between the towers, on the second story, above a row of boutiques and bistros. The waves and white sand beach were just downstairs, but my kids preferred the pool, which was long and narrow, shallow at both ends. They were afraid of jellyfish and sharks, of crabs and eels and stingrays, of the waves tugging at their knees, their ankles. They were afraid of everything that might happen out there in that heaving water even if we, their mother and grandmother, on point for the Beach Patrol, sentried the water's edge, sharp-eyed and attentive as the gulls wheeling in the blue summer sky.

Mom sighed, way louder than necessary.

"We picked this place because of the pool," I told her, tugging at the thread of a conversation we'd been starting and stopping throughout her visit. "We wanted the kids to have that option."

"Options, options," said my mother.

"Marco Polo," I answered.

A pretty, blond lifeguard in a red maillot, a silver whistle hanging from a lanyard around her neck, circled the concrete deck of the pool. She crouched down to say something to the kids. Then the three of them laughed. Sam and Veronica squirted mouth water at each other. They were the only ones in the pool.

"Your kids are scaredy-cats."

"They're not!" I repositioned myself, trying to get comfortable

167

on the lounge, or maybe just protect myself from my mother's target practice. "Read your book."

But Mom kept watching my kids, my silly, lively kids, who were at least as brave as any other kids their ages, six and eight. They wore matching neon-colored bathing suits they'd picked out themselves; trunks for Sam and a two-piece for Veronica. The fabric was printed with hallucinogenic sea creatures, everything they were afraid of in the ocean.

"If you're going to vacation by the ocean, your kids should learn to swim in it."

"They will. In time."

Cool and calm, the good mother, I watched my kids jump and swim and splash each other, Marco Polo, but something burned me from the inside out, Mom zapping me with her stun gun, her theories and philosophies.

"If you want to go down to the beach, Mom, just go. We're not stopping you."

She shrugged. A boom box near the lifeguard's chair played an all-Motown station, the Supremes singing Baby Love; Marvin Gaye and Tammi Tyrell, Ain't No Mountain High Enough.

"You kids were fish, remember?" Mom said. "You'd swim in anything."

Now she was dredging up the past, one of her favorite pastimes, mostly because she could create herself as the heroine of every story, the perfect mother. Though it was true that my sisters and I were fish when we were little. True, too, that my earliest and happiest memories were set in a Cape Cod cottage Daddy built for us on a bluff overlooking the Fore River Shipyard Basin in Weymouth, Massachusetts.

Mom, to hear her tell it—and she told it every chance she got, even to strangers who might, for example, take the lounge chair next to her—had raised her own children, five daughters, to be strong, independent, and self-empowered. Not only were we fish—my girls will swim in anything!—we had, one after the other, earned our Red Cross Lifesaver badges, a critical skill when you grew up near the water. More water when we'd vacationed on Cape Cod, Block Island, and in Atlantic City and Newport; made camping trips to cold, black lakes in upstate New York, New Hampshire, and Vermont and to red cedar lakes in southern New Jersey. Even after Mom and Dad divorced, we visited him in Wellfleet, spent days at Cahoon Hollow or Sandy Neck. So much water so close to home.

Okay, so Mom had raised us to be strong, independent, and self-empowered, whereas my currently absent husband and I were raising our kids to be wimps. We gave in on everything. We always let them have their own way. Plus we gave them everything. Every night, ice cream cones or water ice! And amusement park rides! Every night!

"Don't give them everything," my mother warned me time and again. "You shouldn't give kids everything. They won't learn how to be strong."

Back when we were really little, the ebb and flow of river tides had shaped our days. When the tide was in, we swam in cold, dark water and lay on old blankets on its pebbly shore. It wasn't quite a beach, though my father, every spring, gathered men from the neighborhood to clean the shoreline with rakes and shovels. Then he'd convince one of his connections in city hall to haul in several truckloads of sand. By the end of the summer, the sand would have been washed back into the sea.

When the tide was out, we dug for clams. We feasted on them steamed and dipped in melted butter over newspapers at our outside table. Sometimes, on Friday nights, Mom put them into a chowder. And always, as instructed by my mother, my sisters and I fried our skin under the throbbing sun, slathering it with a pungent concoction of baby oil and iodine that Mom mixed herself. She kept it in an old baby bottle, the crosscut in its rubber nipple releasing orange oil in manageable spurts.

My mother loved the sun. If you knew anything at all about her, you knew she loved the sun. If you knew anything at all about my mother and father together, you knew she loved the sun, and Daddy loved her with a tan—the richer, the more walnutty, the better.

Nightly, after our baths, again instructed by my mother, my sisters and I glazed one another with cleanser from a round, blue jar. It had a soothing eucalyptus scent. We went to bed on sun-dried sheets in just our underpants. Seared by the sun, I used to drift off to sleep, imagining I was on fire, that I glowed. When our skin browned and bubbled, we pulled it off each other's backs in strips.

"Just sayin'," Mom said, her eyes, behind her sunglasses, glued to *The Fulfillment*. "They can't learn if you don't teach them."

"Okay, I get it, Mom. You were a better mother than I am, superior in every way. Hats off to ya'."

Cage match heating up, my husband Doug would say if he were here. He liked to watch. But he wasn't here. He was working in the city and due in late Friday afternoon.

Mom sighed, less dramatically this time. "Let me go make lunch," she said. "Least I can do."

I watched her go, a good-looking woman still; her hair, once brunette, now shimmering silver white. Dignified and self-possessed, despite the depredations of arthritis in her knees and fingers. Her swimsuit was modest and expensive, in a swirling blue-green pattern shot through with metallic threads. A small skirt skimmed the tops of her legs, a style appropriate for older women whose thighs, no matter how thin or fit they might be, begin to look like candles melting. Over it, Mom wore the lacy white cover-up I bought for her at a boutique downstairs. She'd seen it in the window and fallen in love with it. I liked to make her happy. Least I could do.

A few years before, on a similar vacation, at another rental at a different beach, when she'd also come to help while Doug was working, she'd been appalled that my Sam, at three, was still in diapers. It just about killed her that Sam always knew when he was going to have a BM, her acronym of choice. He'd disappear for a few minutes, then return, his fragrant diaper announcing what we'd already figured out, demanding, in his own particular language, to be changed.

"If he can do that, he can certainly use a toilet," she said. "I've watched him and he goes right on schedule. You're way too easy on him."

After that, my mother cornered Sam, captured him, and sat him on the toilet, following the schedule she'd surmised. I have no idea what happened in the bathroom while she sat on the tub's edge waiting, but, by the end of the week, Sam's toilet training was complete. Mom pointed out that he was quite proud of his "ker-plunk." He never had an accident.

"See, I've saved you a fortune in those so-called disposable diapers," she said, triumphant, though I stopped her from tallying up the precise cost of Sam's diaper usage. Score one for Nana, though her relationship with Sam was never quite the same. Sam liked to keep a safe distance between himself and her. Not that she noticed, or cared. She was the grown-up, after all. You shouldn't try to be friends with your children.

Soon enough, Mom reappeared, carrying our lunch on a big melamine tray imprinted with sailboats. She'd reapplied her lipstick, combed her hair. She smiled, the perfect hostess, turning lunch into a party, though the menu was my choice, not hers. Vegetarian hot dogs, organic sweet potato chips, carrot and celery sticks, and chilled bottles of iced green tea. She set everything on a white table beneath a blue and pink umbrella

"Come and get it, yummy, yummy," she called out to Sam and Veronica, who scrambled from the water to the table, dripping chlorinated water, not bothering with towels. Each grabbed a veggie dog and handfuls of the chips.

"Yummy, yummy," Mom repeated, brightly, as I joined them, pulling a chair up to the table.

Of course, Mom did not consider this lunch yummy yummy, but she'd promised, earlier in the week, during an argument at the local grocery store, where we'd searched mostly in vain for good vegetarian food, to keep her mouth shut about what I fed my kids. You're the parent, you get to choose, that's my philosophy, she repeated more times than I could count. Not that I understand it. I don't. Ice cream every night, but no meat. What's wrong with meat? A little chicken breast. Some sirloin tips.

Sam had sidled up to me, the safe place, drenching me with dripping pool water. Watching him chow down, shoving one big hunk after another into his bluish mouth, you could believe that the vegetarian hot dogs were, in fact, yummy yummy.

"Whoa, whoa, slow down." Mom reached, however gently, for his arm. "You're supposed to chew 20 times or more."

Sam looked at me to see if this was true, and I nodded yes. He shrugged.

When he took his next bite, Veronica began to count for him. "One, two, three, four. . . ." She reached 12 before gulping, almost choking on unchewed hunks of her own pup, and collapsed into unfathomable giggles.

"I had to boil them because they wouldn't broil," said Mom. "They just turned black and shriveled up."

"You're not used to cooking veggie meats."

"Veggie meats? Isn't that an oxymoron?" She smiled, proud that she'd lobbed such a fine word at me, oxymoron.

"Soy. They're made from soy. Just read the directions on the package, Mom. I'm pretty sure it says, Do Not Broil."

Mom looked at her own lunch on its bright blue paper plate, a soy hot dog in a wheat bun, smothered in organic ketchup, relish, and mustard. She looked at it as though it threatened to bite her back. But she picked it up and, ever so slowly, bit into it. All three of us watched her. She chewed contemplatively, and I gave her a warning look: Don't say anything negative in front of Sam and Veronica.

"A memory," she murmured, still masticating and looking at her food. "Mmm. That's what it is. A memory."

"A memory?"

"It tastes like a memory of a hot dog," she said. "Not exactly a real hot dog."

"Well, my kids don't have memories of real hot dogs because they've never eaten them."

It just about killed her not to answer. Instead, she gave me one of her looks, an eloquent one that told me—though she barely moved a facial muscle—what a self-righteous elitist I'd turned out to be; me, with my Ph.D. in Comp Lit, my tenured university position. Smarty-pants, I expected her to call me. Because I was no longer just an ordinary know-it-all; I was a professional know-it-all. Got paid for it. To her chagrin. Yes, much to Mom's chagrin. Or so it seemed to me.

"Admit it," she demanded. "Admit that the burgers and franks and fries cooking on the boardwalk downstairs smell wonderful."

"They do, they do, they do," my children chorused. I ignored them. I ignored her. Then Sam and Veronica were done. They raced to the pool's edge and jumped in.

"Wait," wailed my mother, standing, running to the pool's edge. "They're supposed to wait. They might get a cramp."

"Mom," I called, standing now myself, rushing after her. She was so embarrassing sometimes. "Look." I pointed to the pool, which gave off the sharp stench of chlorine. "It's shallow. Even if they do get a cramp, which they won't, I could jump in and rescue them."

"They should play by the rules," Mom cried, so loud that the pretty lifeguard turned to look. "I always made you kids play by the rules."

"What rules? Waiting after eating isn't a rule. It's a suggestion."

"It's a precaution," Mom compromised. "Right? Isn't it a precaution?" she asked the lifeguard, who smiled and nodded yes. "Isn't waiting after eating a sensible precaution?"

The lifeguard nodded and turned away. She wasn't going to get into the middle of us.

"Okay, Mom, it's a precaution," I conceded. "But it's not a rule."

Mom and I went back to our lounge chairs, pink and white like the umbrellas, and also faded by the sun. Mom took off her lacy cover-up and sat with her back to me, reapplying to her calves an SPF 4, the tanning gel she'd begun to use when, on the advice of her doctor, she stepped up from baby oil and iodine. That's when I noticed a knob of darkened skin below her left shoulder blade, a queer asymmetrical extrusion, maybe a quarter of an inch across, with ragged borders, jagged peaks, and deep gullies in variegated shades of gray and black and brown. By instinct, as if it were a ball of fuzz or a black fly, I brushed it with my fingertips. Mom jumped, surprised. Over her shoulder, she looked back at me. I moved in closer, leaning over to peer at it, this frill of flesh half-hidden by the shimmering latex of her swimsuit. Yes, a mole, a big ugly mole, the size of a stink-bug, protruded at the apex of the bodice and the bra strap. A small, dark thing that, I could tell by touching it, had dug deeply into her.

"How long has that been there?" I asked, retreating, taking off my own robe, tossing it onto another lounge, one heaped with towels, the children's sweatshirts, and my novel.

"What? What's been where?" Mom hated that I might know something about her that she didn't know herself.

"That mole. The one below your shoulder blade."

"No mole there that I know of," she answered, and then added, as if it explained everything, "I don't have eyes in the back of my head."

"What happened to them?"

She turned to me with a sly smile, recalling her past power. Back when my sisters and I were growing up, she saw everything. Mom's laser eyes penetrated pockets, purses, and schoolbags; also walls, doors, and the spaces under beds. She saw into the backs of bureau drawers and beneath the scented paper lining them. Yes, my mother was both nearsighted and farsighted. She had eyes every-where. For her, seeing backward was routine.

175

"I don't need them anymore," she said. "What a relief."

I don't get what she meant by this, what a relief. I reached over and put my hand, palm flat, onto her freckled, basting shoulder. With my index finger, Mr. Pointer, I traced down to the mole.

"It's right here," I said, tapping its ferocious surface. "Probably under your bra strap most of the time."

"I can't feel it." She flinched and pulled away. "And I don't have anyone to check my back."

Click. Another button pressed: Mom's loneliness since the divorce, which had happened when I was a teenager, maybe 20 years before. Get over it.

Mom picked up *The Fulfillment* and stretched out on the lounge, her skin slick and coppery.

"Haven't you read that before?"

She nodded yes.

"Why don't you read something new?" I asked, but chomped down on the rest of my sentence before the words escaped—something challenging instead of cheesy romance.

"It's a world I like to go back into every now and then," Mom said, yearning, maybe wistful, like a character from that story, *The Fulfillment*, though I'd never read it. "It's like a vacation. Keep your eye on them, okay?" She nodded toward Sam and Veronica, before turning back to her book.

As if I wouldn't. So I watched my rambunctious kids, less than two years apart in age, which Mom had declared a good thing when I told her of my second, unplanned and unexpected pregnancy. A really good thing, according to her, since I'd waited so long to procreate, and no child should be raised alone. "I was done with all this by the time I was your age," she never tired of reminding me—especially if I mentioned that I was tired; that my children wore me out. My age, 35, at that time. I watched my children, splishing and splashing, fishy out of water, mermaid on the deck, wishing for their energy, at least a little bit of it. Yet I pondered Mom's forever lamentation, her loneliness since Dad left her oh so long ago. It rippled outward, like the water, when the kids were cannonballing. Or maybe it seeped like water into me. When I was with her, I couldn't get away from it, me with my extended education, my Red Cross Lifesaver badge.

No, my mother did not have anyone to check her back, had not for many years. Not that she'd ever tried to find anyone after Daddy left. After Daddy left, she never dated again. At first, she was too busy raising us. Her claim. Then she announced, again to anyone who'd listen, "I'm a one-man woman. . . ."She took pride in this belief, that she was a one-man woman even though her ex, Daddy, was clearly not a one-woman man.

Mom stayed behind in that Cape Cod cottage on the water. She stayed alone in the house we'd grown up in. Stayed there without anyone to check her back. Still she loved the sun, still loved living near the beach, but her gleaming, burnished skin—the skin Daddy once had loved—began mottling and wrinkling. Over the years, pleats gathered at her elbows and her knees; a baleful sac drooped under her chin. Crow's feet ruched the edges of her eyes. Many people told me my mother was still beautiful. What a shame she's alone. And I suppose it was true, that she was still beautiful, and it was a shame she was alone. But she was a one-man woman, that's what my mother was, and that one man was gone. Into another life, another marriage.

So Mom lived alone. In recent years, many years now, as my sisters and I started our own families, she spent weeks at a time staying with one of us or another, a carpetbagger, "jetting" as my sisters and I put it, up and down the Eastern Seaboard on our dime. She took turns at our houses. Three weeks in Hilton Head; a month in Cundy's Harbor; Christmas in Stowe, at the Trapp Family Inn. Poor Mom! we giggled to each other whenever she tried to throw a pity party for herself. Of course I loved her, we all did. We, I, loved having her around. But sometimes her never-ending sadness worked my last nerve.

Daddy had no such trouble moving on. He moved on to other jobs and wives and homes, each of the latter larger than the last. I thought of Daddy's homes as nesting houses, like Russian dolls, each hidden in a larger one, except for the first one, the smallest, where Mom had stayed, and which could never be pried open and nothing else could ever fit inside it.

As for Daddy's wives, all were more or less the same size and shape, slim-hipped and large-breasted, like my mother once had been. The wives were the same size, more or less, but each one was younger, newer, and shinier than the last one. Unlike Daddy's houses, the newer wives did not become larger and, hence, capable of containing all the others. Instead, each seemed tighter, smoother, harder, and less capable of opening. The most recent is a few years younger than I. She has yet to reproduce. She never will.

Mom dragged her feet until it was almost Christmas, even though I'd clued in all my sisters, and all of us got on her case. At last she went to the dermatologist who did an immediate biopsy. She told no one until she got the results: malignant melanoma. That small dark thing had bitten into her long ago. Right after that, surgeons cut a hunk out of her back, tissue all around the mole. Then they went back for more. Stage IV.

Mom blamed me for noticing the mole, as if, by pointing it out to her, I'd put it there. That hideous tumor.

"You should mind your own goddamned business," she said, enraged, when she found out that I'd told my sisters, which I'd done as soon as I got home from our vacation. Yes, I called them all, and enlisted their help in getting her to see a doctor as soon as possible. Instead of appreciating my concern, Mom blamed me, Dr. Smarty Pants, for "ruining my life." That's what she said in that last phone call before she stopped speaking to me altogether. She told my sisters that she would have preferred not to know. She would have preferred ignorance.

Just before Easter, when Mom went into the hospital for what turned out to be the last time, she was still giving me the silent treatment. My sisters couldn't knock her out of it. Even Doug tried. No dice. "Shoot the messenger," he said after she hung up on him, too.

For weeks, I stumbled around the cage, wary of its boundaries, its barbed wire. I couldn't find my fighting partner. I couldn't find a way out.

According to Mom's wishes, her caregivers affixed to her chart and her headboard a fluorescent orange sticker scrawled with the letters DNR—Do Not Resuscitate. During those last days, between the pain of the metastases, the pain meds, and exhaustion, Mom's moments of lucidity were few. That's when I took a chance. Humble, remorseful—Why had I opened my big mouth? Why had I pointed out that mole?—I walked out of the cage. I went to the hospital and took my turn with my sisters, sitting with Mom, holding her hand, whispering stories, and humming songs. My beautiful mother, shriveled now, her skin the texture of an old boot, unrecognizable except for her shimmering crown of white hair.

Once, when I was alone with her, she woke up and asked for water, but was too weak to sip it through the straw. I put some ice chips into her mouth, with my hands, the ice melting between my fingers and her lips. I wiped the dribbles up with a soft cloth, and then I kissed her mouth.

"Annie," she said, her voice a raspy whisper. "Oh, Annie, you're such a sweet girl. You always have been. Thank you so very much."

Annie is my youngest sister.

From her hospital room, I could look down at the water of Quincy Bay and the Fore River. In the far distance, I could see the enormous rusted edifices, the cranes, catwalks, and scaffoldings of the shipyard, now shuttered and abandoned, where both Mom and Dad had worked. Where they met, and began to date, just after World War II. Mom had been a billing clerk; Dad, a naval architect. Mom, of course, stopped working once the war was over and she married.

Looking down toward the water, I knew that if I swam the river backward, it would bring me to that Cape Cod cottage where we'd grown up, the house Daddy built for us on the bluff above the river, and then abandoned. Where Mommy ended up living alone. Still I had trouble believing what the doctor said, that Mom's melanoma, one of the slowest growing of cancers, had begun back then, during those radiant hot days when we laughed and swam and sunned ourselves by the water. And now, during the final round of our struggle, Mom neither beat nor overpowered me, know-it-all that I am, me, with my degrees, my Red Cross Lifesaver's badge.

She just erased me. I was gone, and soon she would be, too.

One day, on my way to Mom's hospice room, I glimpsed Daddy's new wife in a waiting room, fiddling with her rings and bracelets. I was not surprised, then, to see him, in a pinstriped suit, his tie ever-so-slightly loosened, slumped in a chair at the foot of Mom's bed.

"He's here for us," emphasis on "us," one of my sisters, maybe Karen, maybe Rebecca, announced before I'd even asked the question. Then Mom, as if she'd picked up his scent, or felt him shifting in his seat, opened her eyes. She saw him there, leaning forward, as if about to speak to her.

"Is that Daddy?" A smile flitted across her face. "Did Daddy come home?"

Nobody answered her, but Mom seemed satisfied. She closed her eyes and went back to sleep, her smile, a memory, still flickering across her once-beautiful face. She didn't speak again.

DANCING WITH NED

IT WAS A STEAMY AUGUST RUSH HOUR when they left the Granite State, three of them, Cancer Queenie, Husband, and Big Sis, heading to the heart of Beantown, some 75 miles away. Husband drove the couple's Cherokee, and beside him, in the bucket seat, Queenie held in her slender hands a Rubber Maid container with a blue lid, purchased in bulk at Costco, for times such as this, when Queenie was in transit, nausea inevitable, and sinks and/or toilets as unreachable as moon or stars.

Husband, a contractor, an authentic Mr. Fix-It, white-knuckled the leather-wrapped steering wheel, hunched over it, ramming through battalions of Expeditions, Armadas, Hummers, Rogues, Explorers, Excursions on the glimmering tangle of superhighways surrounding the metropolis. Queenie held her bucket, hunched too; looking into the bucket, not at the apocalyptic streams of vehicles on merges, entrance and exit ramps, cloverleaves; arteries that supplied the city's great heart, often clogging it, and that might, at any moment trigger an infarction.

Big Sis sat in back, steaming mad but pretending she was fine with her demotion to 'along for the ride.' She, after all, should have been the one behind the wheel, taking her sister to Brigham and Women's for this appointment with one of the great gurus of gynecological cancer. That had been the original plan. That's why she, Big Sis, Celestine, had been summoned from Philadelphia: to drive Queenie to see this oncologist whom she'd waited months to see.

"Oh, Cellie, please, please come. I need you to drive me to see … *pretty please with sugar on it."* Queenie's exhortations slipped through fiber optic cables, a caress.

Husband worked in construction and had to finish a big job. *"He'll be knee-deep in doo-doo; maybe even get fired, if he doesn't meet this deadline."*

You got it, said Big Sis keeping the promise she'd made to herself three years before when Queenie, aka Ruth Ann, got her diagnosis, ovarian cancer, stage 3B or 4. She'd do anything within her power to help her sister through her illness. Hence, Big Sis dropped everything, work, children, other responsibilities, too numerous to name, and, hopped into her Sentra. She began on I-95, speeding 316 miles north and then east along shivering swaths of highways, doing better than 70 mph most of the way. Eyes adhered to the shimmering roadway ahead as she blasted Sade's Lovers Rock, and chomped on a sustaining mix of almonds, walnuts, raisins, dried apricots chopped into little pieces, plus M&Ms. Again and again, her fingers wriggled through the Baggie on her lap until they found the M&Ms, always in the bottom corners of the bag. Her beloved sister, Cancer Queenie, had begged Big Sis to make the trip. (It was Big Sis herself who had baptized her sister Cancer Queenie, noting her sudden uncharacteristic querulousness, her peevish grumbling, her regal expectations, her imperious demands. Queenie had smacked her cheek, then laughed and couldn't stop.)

Outside it was hot, hot, hot. Inside the Cherokee, a chill wind blew, Freon tinged air laced too with anger, confusion and uncertainty, mashed up feelings, not all yet identifiable. On sleep dep, Big Sis gazed out at the awful traffic, annoyed, no, disappointed, no, angry, no incensed about sitting in the back instead of driving Queenie. All through the 300-plus miles she'd driven the day before, she thought about her upcoming day with Queenie, no husbands, no kids, just the two of them, the way it used to be. Not lunch and a movie, true, nor a shopping trip to an upscale discount mall, but still, a girl's day, the two of them together. Sisters, secret sharers.

No reason given for the change of plans. Don't ask; don't tell had always been the Couple's policy. Today, Big Sis adopted it. She took her seat in back as if it were the best possible vantage point from which to experience the world. She zipped her lips, tried to quiet her roiling gut, and sparred with Queenie's dread, which felt like her own, suffocating in the heat.

Queenie's trip, this really bad trip, had begun in the most mundane possible way. She'd gone to her local emergency room complaining of indigestion, maybe poisoning from some bad lobster pie the night before, or too much chardonnay. She ended up diagnosed with advanced ovarian cancer. The emergency room doctor had dialed up the on-call surgeon who showed up in a flash. He cut her from hip to hip. He discovered long, tangled strands of tumor wound around her ovaries, her fallopian tubes, her uterus, her large and small intestines. Epithelial ovarian carcinoma.

Since then, in the most cliché but also most apt of tropes, she'd waged a high tech war against the wily mutant that had taken her unaware, rooting in her omentum, a fatty apron covering the belly that holds the stomach, intestines, other organs in place. The omentum, a nurturing place for mutant cells. It sloughed them off and they fell like acid rain into nearby tissues, rooting, creating more tumor sites, more malignancies. The pitched battle to out-smart it: cutting edge forms of radiation and multiple surgeries — debulking for fuck's sake. Early on, Queenie had been debulked. *Some diet plan*, Queenie joked, shriveling from a size 12 to a size 6, snap, just like that. *You're svelte, dahling, svelte*, Big Sis insisted. *You've always wanted to be svelte.*

What damned good does that do me now? Queenie wailed.

For a full year Queenie had worn a colostomy bag, a fucking bag of shit attached forever to her body, and Husband often helped to change it. *Doesn't that prove his deep true undying love?* Queenie had asked Big Sis more than once, and Big Sis always answered yes.

Yes, Husband had been there every step, through all the ups and downs but now, in an inversion of his truest and best self, a mellow guy, an aging hippie loved with all her heart by Queenie, he'd become prone to irritability, outbreaks of rage. He'd developed tics. All of a sudden, for no reason whatsoever, he'd blink a bunch of times, like he was trying to keep his eyeballs in their sockets. After that, he'd stretch out his lower jaw, as if preparing to take a big bite out of something, maybe an Italian hero sandwich, or possibly a Baconator, one of his favorites, despite its proven negative health consequences. Then he'd jerk his head two or three times to the left, with a startled look, disbelief, a grappling with reality, or a pitched battle to fight it off. At times, during this ritual, he made a growling sound.

In the Cherokee, in the awful heat and traffic, Queenie smacked him every time he twitched.

"When did you develop Tourette's Syndrome?" she asked, as if it were an unprecedented inquiry, not one she'd made at least a dozen times before.

"Tourette's? I don't have Tourette's." He clutched the wheel tighter, hunched lower.

"Maybe it's dyskinesia," said Queenie, an avid student of the PDR. "You know, tardive dyskinesia. What meds are you taking?"

He turned to her, ignoring eight lanes of traffic gleaming in front of them. "No dyskinesia," he said. "Whatever that is." He blinked three times, then twitched.

"Involuntary spastic movements of the face," announced Queenie. "Often a side effect of anti-psychotic medication."

"I don't take anti-psychotic medication."

"Then why do you keep spazzing like that? I really hate it. You look ridiculous."

"Like what?"

She pointed to Husband's chin as his head jerked to the left.

"You blink and stick out your jaw and then you jerk your head."

Big Sis watched their routine, the oh-so familiar tango of their love, a dreary back and forth of accusation and denial, one they'd been doing their entire married life, a quarter of century, neither of them knowing how to stop or change the steps.

"It's not involuntary," insisted Husband. "I'm doing it on purpose. It's relaxing." Then he jerked his head back the other way.

"You look ridiculous," repeated Queenie, shaking her own head.

"It feels good. It beats getting hooked on Xanax."

This last, Big Sis understood, was a dig at Queenie who'd been known, from time to time, through the years and decades, during periods of extreme duress, to rely upon the occasional benzodiazepine in order to calm down. OK, Queenie was a hypo-chondriac, many of her loved ones, even Big Sis, at times whispered behind her back. Much as Big Sis loved her, her love notwithstand-ing, Queenie was a card-carrying hypochondriac, the card being her Health Benefits Prescription Drug Plan ID. Queenie's kitchen cabinet, where she also kept coffee and corn flakes, was a satellite site of the US pharmacopeia: rows of translucent brown, white-capped containers, arranged the way most women organize their spices; so many pills, so little time. Chronic fatigue, Epstein-Barre, Lyme's disease, IBS, fibromyalgia, possibly lupus — Queenie suf-fered from them all.

Most every summer, when the heat and the kids and the gen-eral demands and frustrations of life got to be too much, when she tired of hiking and camping with her boys, and sewing and reading, and arguing with Husband, Queenie took to her bed. For days on end. *You've got the vapors, honey,* Big Sis liked to tease. *You know, like our great-grandmother who struggled with the vapors her entire life. All 83 years of it.*

"Hmmmph," Queenie replied to Husband in the Cherokee. "Try the Xanax. It might help."

Cancer Couple lived in a quaint New Hampshire town, in a 1950s rancher they'd rescued from ruin, on a quiet Tree Named street without sidewalks. Picture perfect, this town, with its white-stee-pled churches, and a landscaped central square where, from dawn until dusk, Old Glory flapped from a tall pole. The square, more of a circle, really, bejeweled by coffee shops, antique shops, an honest-to-goodness hardware store, a used bookstore, stores with glass-paned doors and crystal doorknobs.

Along the edge of town, not quite through it, rushed the Merrimack River, black and shiny, narrow though deep, swift-moving, its sighs and gurgles, its endless headlong race, audible always throughout town, except during the darkest months of winter when it was frozen, its ruffles of white water, its slithering currents stopped in time.

Wired and tired, Big Sis had reached town about nightfall, slowed along the spiraling exit ramp, slowed more on the narrow street through the center, circling the square, her mind still stuck in the slipstream, somewhere back on I-495.

Oh, Cellie, please, please come. I need you.

She pulled up in front of the couple's rancher. It glowed from the inside, a clean, well-lighted place. She got out, stretched, then hurried to the salvaged glass-paned back door. Big Sis tried the door, found it locked, then banged on the glass. She waited an eternity, knocked again.

Husband at last appeared, a sad beaten man. Big Sis watched him shuffle to the door, unlock and open it.

"Oh, you," he said.

Husband pointed in the direction of their brand new Florida room, then disappeared, a relief to Big Sis, since the last time she'd visited Husband had called her *the most insensitive, self-centered person on the face of the earth.* A furious, red-faced, spit-flecked accusation that had sent Big Sis packing. She'd grabbed her things, gotten into her car and driven back to New Jersey. Husband would repeat his assessment of Big Sis, with variations, throughout Queenie's illness, even with Queenie stuck there, inside Cancerland's ever-spinning door of terror and elation, one she could neither stop nor exit.

"Yo, Ruthie," hollered Big Sis, heading for the new room. "Oh, Cellie," Queenie cried, "you're here."

The Couple had built this room — they called it the Florida room, Florida, with its connotations of citrus fruit, sunshine, sun-heated skin, beaches, retirement, both the Gulf and the Atlantic, easily accessible — the year before, soon after Queenie's cancer had gone into remission and her oncologists had declared her cancer free.

Cancer free!!

Yeah, baby, I beat the rap, Queenie chorused every chance she got, her eyes optimistic blue, a smile cracking her pretty, hope-lit face. *Life goes on.*

Dodged a bullet, echoed Husband.

With its skylights and big windows, the Florida room looked out onto the Couple's sloping yard, edged with tall white pines. Outside, they'd built a patio, its focal point a gas grill, *big as an APC,* Husband bragged. They'd be spending long years together here, Cancer Couple would. They'd grow old together, entertaining grandchildren, grilling steak, chicken and hot dogs, or inside watching crime shows on the big flat screen. In winter, they'd watch the snow falling on the pines.

Queenie sat in her La-Z-Boy recliner, a brand new one in a jazzy geometric print, the Incredible Shrinking Woman, so pale; her skin milky but with a bluish tinge, like fat free milk. A doll in a too big chair. A pink cap over her bald head, pink sweats, extra small, but still too big, draping like a toga on her torso and her thighs. Brown Uggs on her feet despite the August heat. A remote in her little hand, several more beside her on the table. A pilot navigating a trip she was taking by herself. The Iron Chef seared soft-shell crabs in a shiny silver pan.

Inside this shrinking woman, Big Sis saw the sister she'd grown up with, so smart, so funny; robust and rowdy, a brunette with sapphire eyes, a size 10 at her thinnest; a 12 most of the time, but firm-fleshed, with the heart-shaped ass all the Malloy girls shared. The sister she adored. In college, the same Catholic college, a Jesuit school, Big Sis and Queenie caroused around the bars of Boston and Newport; guzzling Dubonnet Red on the rocks with a twist, just for the hell of it; yakking forever; laughing their heads off about nothing. They'd doubled-dated with their future husbands, gotten married the same year, just a few months apart, each serving as the other's maid of honor. "A Chinaman and a Jew," said their mother. "Go figure."

Queenie, hypnotized by the Iron Chef, didn't look up when Big Sis walked in. "Sit, sit," she commanded, eyes riveted to the flailing crustaceans. She patted the arm of the recliner next to her, Husband's spot.

"You sure?"

"Sit. He'll never know. He's done for the night."

Big Sis lowered her butt into the matching recliner, but feeling, as she did, Husband's territoriality, his disinclination to have anyone, let alone Big Sis, lower their fat ass, heart-shaped or otherwise, down on his throne. The crabs jumped and sizzled in the pan. Queenie remained mute, mesmerized by this luscious fantasy of food. She had not so much as a bite for the best part of a year. Instead, she'd been nourished by a creamy vitamin-laden goo called TPN, purchased by the quart in sterile Baggies, and shot into her bloodstream through a titanium port above her clavicle, following the same route as the chemo. Queenie didn't ask her how she was, how her trip had gone. Silent too, Sis watched her watching. Since her recurrence,

Queenie was like that sometimes, mute and ethereal, off in her own world. Big Sis hoped it was peaceful there, but she couldn't ask — since Queenie refused to admit she ever slipped away.

After Iron Chef, Queenie, commandeering the multiple remotes, a woman of agency, of power, they watched reruns of NYPD Blue. Sis took Queenie's hand, feeling the small bones, bird bones, plus itsy-bitsy tendons, veins and arteries, encased within her soft silky skin. Enchanted, Big Sis and Queenie watched Andy and Bobby on the big screen, *fabulous color, incredible definition,* rounding up mutts and humps and skels and perps. Giggling and sighing over Bobby, they fell backward, 20 or 30 years, to the place where their entwined futures had glistened, not a shadow anywhere.

"I've always had the hots for him." Queenie spoke sorrowfully, that part of her life over before she was ready to let it go. She gestured with a remote to Bobby. "How bout you?"

"I wouldn't kick him out of bed."

"Heh-heh, I knew it," Queenie cackled, a hint of her old sexy self. "Sometimes when we were doing it, you know, back when we were still doing it, when I had functional parts left to do it with, I imagined I was Kim Delaney banging Bobby. That crazed lust."

A necessary fantasy, thought Big Sis as Queenie's attention stayed riveted to the screen, on Jimmy Smits, in his NYPD Blue glory, a man to whom Husband could not ever measure up. Not for a second, not even from his best angle, on his best day. Which, in the opinion of Big Sis, had lasted maybe only for a nanosecond, back in the '80s, a speck of time just long enough to snag Queenie, and long since passed. Queenie could have done so much better.

Queenie sighed. A single tear trickled down her cheek. She was already far away.

In the morning, after hardly sleeping, feeling she was in a foreign land whose culture she didn't understand, whose language she could not rely on, Big Sis gathered up the items they needed for their journey: Rubbermaid container with lid; wet wipes; wintergreen Lifesavers; bottles of water; a soft pillow in case Queenie's bony butt began to hurt. She was putting them into the Jeep when Husband re-appeared, freshly shaven, his hair wet from the shower. He held up the keys, jangled them before her, like they'd been playing a game and he'd won.

"I'll be driving," he said. He turned to Queenie. "Let's go, or we'll be late."

Big Sis watched him walk out into the driveway and climb into the driver's seat, turn on the ignition. Queenie, leaning on her walker, stood in the open doorway of the house looking at a sparrow perched on what was left of the pots of red and white petunias Big Sis had planted for her that spring. "I love you so much, Cellie," Queenie said.

Then, bearing much of Queenie's weight, what little of it there was, Big Sis helped Queenie clomp over to the Jeep and climb into it.

Boston rush hour traffic: Arterial sclerosis all around the city, the poor old city, its streets laid out eons before the Expedition or the Hummer or even the little Cherokee could have been envisioned. A madness...Time ticked past. For a while, Lucinda Williams spoke for them. Car Wheels on a Gravel Road; 2 Kool 2 B 4 Gotten; Can't Let Go. But then Queenie began to fret that they'd be late. "Could you step on it, please?" She skewered Husband with a look.

"I'm stepping. Chill," he answered. Blink blink.

The hospital, a magisterial place of hope and future, shone in the distance, a city on the hill, shimmering in the morning light, but they could not seem to reach it. Between the grid of one-way streets, the mess of the Big Dig, the traffic and the heat, Husband began cursing, a throaty mumble, *fucking shit, goddamn assholes, motherfuckers...*

"That's another sign of Tourette's." Queenie's voice was edged with triumph. "That cursing." Then she puked into the Rubbermaid, a grinding sound, like an unprimed pump.

Big Sis reached both arms around the front seat. With one, she handed her sister a wet wipe; with the other, caressed Queenie's bony shoulder. Queenie's anxiety, a scaled and heavy thing, slithered up through her palm. Big Sis grasped it, sensed its danger

"You're an idiot, you know that, right?" Husband aimed his tirade to Big Sis in the rearview mirror. "This is all your fault." Queenie's puking, he meant but did not say.

That morning, cuddled next to Queenie on the loveseat in the Florida room, still pretending they were like they used to be, not just sisters, but best friends, their lives a bowl of cherries, scads of happiness, their birth right, piling up around them, Big Sis had eaten breakfast, a cup of strong Green Mountain breakfast blend with light cream, and a toasted, butter-slathered English muffin. Queenie moaned over the smell of the coffee, the toasted muffin.

"How about a teeny-tiny little sip? A little crumb?" Big Sis coaxed. She held the mug up to her sister's mouth. Queenie inhaled the steamy fumes but didn't drink. Then she took the English muffin out of Big Sis's hands. Queenie held it, stroked its edges with her fingertips the way she always fingered fine bone china — she collected antique cups and saucers — because she loved the way it felt. Queenie sniffed the muffin. Her pink tongue flicked out and back. She licked the butter melted in one of the muffin's little crannies. A taste, an itsy-bitsy but oh so scrumptious taste! Minutes later, paroxysms of nausea, green bile spewing, a force that knocked her to her hands and knees onto the brand new tiled floor. Big Sis got down beside her, the two of them on all fours. Big Sis held on to Queenie until the spasms passed and the spurts of green bile stopped.

"How stupid can you get?" Husband asked when he'd walked in, seen his wife sprawled on the floor and Big Sis cleaning up. "You know she can't eat."

"It's not her fault," cried Queenie. "Stop picking on her. I hate it when you two fight."

Now, in the Cherokee, stalled in traffic-pocalyps, the world no doubt ending soon, Queenie didn't say a word. Neither did Big Sis.

When at last they reached the hospital, all perspective disappeared. They could not actually see the building. Instead, they entered through a series of concrete chutes, hard and lightless, a tunnel, spiraling deeper, into an underground garage. As they nosed downward, three levels or more, a choked pitchy sound filled the Cherokee, a whine, a wail, a wounded animal on board. No, Queenie. Husband ignored her, pretended he couldn't hear. He couldn't allow himself to hear. Had to find a parking space. Big Sis sopped up the sobs. She reached around the seat to hold her sister's shoulders.

Finally Husband found a handicapped spot near an elevator, Level 3C, Big Sis made a mental note, then, on second thought, scribbled their location in her day planner. Husband hopped out, grabbed one of the wheelchairs lined up near the elevator door like carts outside a supermarket. Big Sis got out, too. She opened Queenie's door, stood there stroking Queenie's soft cheek, ready to lift her into the chair.

Queenie clutched Big Sis's arm, as if she'd been waiting for this chance to divulge critical information. She pulled Big Sis close. "I'm so sorry, Cellie," she whispered. "But he doesn't want you here. Just in case you didn't pick up the vibe."

"Well, I did, honey. I picked it up."

"We had a big fight this morning. He didn't want you to come with us, but I insisted. I mean, after all, you'd driven up from New Jersey, right? He said, 'So what,' but I held my ground."

Why didn't you call me and tell me to stay home? This question thrashed in Big Sis's mouth, but she couldn't ask it. Queenie's face, so close, was paper white, her big eyes sapphire blue.

"No worries," Big Sis said. "I'll do anything for you."

In the underground garage, the weight of the city bore down on them. Big Sis looked at Queenie. That morning, before they left, they'd struggled with grooming and dressing, these sisters had, the older one forcing the younger into the shower, then massaging her feet with a lotion redolent of melon and cucumber; bustling into the laundry room to find something 'halfway decent' for Queenie to wear out into the world. Queenie resisted. She didn't want the shower. She wanted to stay in her pink sweats and Uggs.

I'm comfy. I've gotta right to be comfy, don't I? Don't I have a right to decide about my own clothes? Who the hell cares what I look like?

You're a professional. You've got advanced degrees, for heaven's sake, Big Sis reminded her. *Where's your pride?*

In the toilet, Queenie answered.

Very funny, Big Sis scolded, at last convincing Queenie to 'at least pretend' that she lived somewhere other than Cancerland. That she carried dual citizenship, was not a full-time resident of the crazed place with its ever-spinning doors. Big Sis coaxed Queenie into denim capris, sandals, and a white shirt knotted at her waist to take up the extra slack. Big Sis wrapped Queenie's sweet bald head in a red silk scarf, printed with a pattern of the children of the world. Queenie perked up when Sis waved the scarf in front of her, then tied it into a neat turban. Queenie loved the scarf, a gift from her special ed students at a tri-lingual middle school in Lowell.

But now, on Level 3C, in the dank underground garage, it has slipped down on one side, to where Queenie's eyebrow used to be.

"He says you can't come in the room with us when we meet with the doctor," Queenie said. "He put his foot down on that point. I want you there, but he doesn't."

Big Sis straightened out the scarf, stroked Queenie's cheek.

"It's not personal," said Queenie. "We just don't need any more confusion. That's what he said. No more confusion. No more opinions. We don't need to have anybody else in on the act. It's all too stressful as it is."

Queenie gazed at Big Sis with her baby blues. The humid heat and airless stink of the garage made it hard to breathe. Another time, another place, Big Sis might have argued. Might've asked, *Why did you let me make this trip if he doesn't want me around?* Or, *Why does he get a vote? It's your illness, not his.* Instead, she chirped, "I get that. I can go with that. I'll wait in the waiting room, baby, that's what they're for, right? I'll read my book." Carson McCuller's *The Heart is a Lonely Hunter* for the Southern Lit class she was teaching.

Husband returned with the wheelchair. He and Big Sis helped

Queenie into it. "I can't breathe," she gasped as they waited for the elevator. "No air in here."

"You're hyperventilating," Big Sis said. "It's the anxiety. Breathe normally, nice and slow. Let's count. Breathe in, one...breathe out... " The elevator arrived, they boarded, began ascending, gliding upward to the 20-something floor, up, up, up, as if being pulled up to a deity, one they'd bow before, praying he would, could, stop Queenie's rush toward death.

"I hope he knows more than those clowns at Dartmouth-Hitchcock," Husband said. He made a fist, punched the elevator railing a couple of times. "Those guys were really bad."

Queenie nodded her agreement. Her illness was never supposed to come to this. This recurrence was not supposed to happen. Rage, disappointment, the belief they'd been betrayed, perhaps lied to, trembled on the faces of Cancer Couple as the elevator glided up. Why, only the year before, Queenie had been given a clean bill of health by oncologists considered among the best in the business.

After that three-year long hard fought hell, they'd been told they won, and they believed it. They'd earned it, after all. They were winners. Queenie, one of the lucky ones, was good to go for a normal middle-aged, middle-class lifestyle and life span. She'd gone back to work, they built the addition. *I beat the rap,* Queenie told everyone who'd listen, repeating what she believed the oncs had told her. *Outta Cancerland and back to life.*

Dodged a bullet, husband chorused.

The elevator doors slid open onto a pristine space lined with big windows and a view of vast empty sky. The waiting room, filled with sofas and chairs nicer than any Queenie or Big Sis had ever owned. Not a magazine in sight. No waiting patients either. No indication whatsoever of what could be gotten here. Sit. Take a load off. Relax. Keep your mind off why you're here.

Husband checked his watch. "10:30, right on time. Perfect. I knew it would take three hours."

Just then a set of doors swung open, and a young Asian doctor, his face stricken, rushed toward them.

"You're here, you're here at last," he cried, his arms outstretched like a priest's during the Consecration. "We'd almost given up on you."

"We're right on time," declared Husband, pointing to his Timex, its glowing hands. Blink, blink. Shrug.

"No, 10 a.m.," the doctor said. "Ten." By now his face was scarlet, and he rubbed the pockets of his lab coat. Cancer Couple had kept the Big Guy waiting. This, however, was not the Big Guy, just one of his acolytes.

"Gee, I wonder who screwed that up." Husband aimed his microwave smile at Queenie.

"Chemo brain," she said, two pink spots glowing on her white cheeks.

"No harm done," said the resident, who was young and plump and very serious. Gesturing with a white-sleeved arm, he ushered Cancer Couple, Husband pushing Queenie in the wheelchair, back through the swinging doors. That's when Queenie twisted, turned to give Big Sis the eye. A signal. Big Sis read it, slipped through the swinging doors behind them, into a carpeted hallway done in such soft neutrals that it was hard to tell where the walls ended and the floor began. The carpeting muffled the steady hum of the building's HVAC systems, as well as the gasps and sighs that leaked from Queenie.

Queenie wants me here; needs me here, Big Sis prepared herself to argue. That's when she when she figured out Queenie's ruse. Husband was never not going to drive her to this appointment. But she needed Big Sis there. A last they entered a large light-filled corner office. The resident took a seat in a small chair beside, not behind, the shiny desk and began to interrogate Queenie. He wrote her answers on a yellow legal pad attached to a clipboard.

"On a scale of one to ten, one being the worst, and ten the best, how would you describe your quality of life?"

"My quality of life?" Queenie cried. "Minus ten." She glared at him. "It totally sucks. I never thought I'd ever have to live here, in downtown Bitesville, where everything sucks."

"Bitesville?" repeated the resident.

"The capital of Cancerland." Queenie gazed at him, daring him to challenge her. He didn't, instead wrote on his pad.

"Can't eat or drink. Can't run. Can't play. Can't even love my baby." She tilted her head toward Husband. "But I'm not ready to die. I'm only 47 years old, for heaven's sake. Forty-seven."

"Forty-seven," Husband repeated, outraged, blinking and nodding, agitated, like he was at the customer service counter of a big box store, disputing a warranty.

The resident nodded, too, his smooth brow furrowed, then went back to writing.

"We've sent down all the test results," Husband said, losing patience, taking over. "MRIs, CATs, ultrasounds, blood tests, etcetera, etcetera, etcetera. You must've gotten them. I'm sure you did. You had to have gotten them. From Dartmouth-Hitchcock. All new. All of them recent. And if you looked at them, even a quick glance, you would have noticed what they said: No evidence of disease. N.E.D. She ought to be able to eat."

Husband gestured to his wife who watched him, nodding, encouraging him with her saucer eyes. "Do they know what they're doing up there? I think not! No evidence of disease, but my poor wife still cannot eat, not even a tiny mouthful, without tectonic nausea and the shits. She keeps losing weight."

Big Sis had never before heard her brother-in-law use such vocabulary, such syntax. Behind his thick bifocals, his eyes were wet. She guessed he must have practiced.

"That's why we're here," said Queenie in her normal person voice. "It's what we've got to figure out."

The young resident nodded, made a note. Then he stood, placed his pen carefully into the lapel pocket of his lab coat. "Our imaging devices are excellent," he said suddenly, his mouth pinched, the clipboard clutched to his chest, his other hand on the door. "Unfortunately, technology can't always keep up with the disease."

"What the hell's that supposed to mean?" Husband asked the closing door. "Technology can't always keep up with the disease? Jesus."

Then he turned his gimlet eye on Big Sis.

"I want her here," said Queenie. "She stays. She can take notes."

Queenie handed Big Sis a little pad of paper and a pen. *Teachers Make the World Go 'Round* it said in letters printed around a globe shaped like an apple. Below, in Queenie's looping scrawl, were questions:

Food — when will I eat again?

Surgery for blockage — when? where? length of recovery?

New Protocol? What besides Carbo/Taxol?

Prognosis : Howlong? Howlong? Howlong? Howlong?

Big Sis read this last question as howling. Howling. Howling.

A wail, a keening, a siren sound from deep inside her heart. Queenie, who knew exactly where she stood. Howling. How long? Big Sis clutched her hand. Queenie squeezed back.

For a moment, waiting for the big guy, Big Sis took in the heat-misted Boston skyline. Had it been New York or Philly, cities she knew well, maybe she could've gotten her bearings. But in Boston, Boston of all places, the city of her childhood, home to generations of her, their, ancestors, she was disoriented, lost. She did not recognize any of the tall buildings; couldn't tell where was north or south.

She was still wondering when the Renowned Oncologist himself swept in, his white coat rustling. All three quaked a little. He was tall and thin, with an aquiline nose, austere features, the fingers of a pianist. Better educated, *probbly*, than the three of them put together, thought Big Sis. All the smart successful guys were tall and thin, graceful like that. Beneath his lab coat, his collar was unbuttoned, his silk tie loosened. He carried Queenie's file, a thick one with charts and documents and transparencies sticking out here and there, as though it had been dropped, shoved back together in a rush. Queenie's file, a hot mess, like her failing body, stuffed with things that didn't belong; would not fit, most of them incomprehensible except to an elite highly specialized few. A fluorescent green tab bore her name in big hand-printed letters: Ruth Ann Malloy Quinn.

The oncologist carried Queenie's file and he carried, too, his reputation as one of the world's foremost experts in gynecological cancers. It surrounded him, a shimmering aura that inflated to fill the room. Queenie could hardly breathe. Again she panted, edged toward panic. Big Sis saw this. *Slow it down,* she whispered. She squeezed her sister's hand harder, but she and Husband, too, were having trouble breathing. They gazed at Him, all three, and saw, attached to Him, like flare pins on the vests of waitpersons, the aprons of home improvement store employees, their own anguished optimism, their delirious faith, their bright and gaudy hopes, every last one. Oh yes, this man could — *Say it, he would* — vaporize those renegade cells feeding off the most girl parts of Queenie. He could, *he would,* release Queenie from her illness. He would — *he would, he must* — tell them how to make her well.

He shook each of their hands, spending a couple of extra seconds with Queenie, gazing into her eyes, stroking her shoulder. Then he took his seat behind his desk, rolled his shirtsleeves up to his elbows.

"What do you want from me?" he asked Queenie, his gray eyes full of knowledge if not wisdom. *Believe it, yes, this great oncologist really did want to know.* And he was going to listen, however long it took, their own tardiness notwithstanding. "What can I do for you?"

Simple questions, logical questions, but also as vast and impossible to answer as the sky outside.

That's when Big Sis realized, and perhaps to Cancer Couple, too, that they'd reached a pinnacle of the health care system, a place above bed pans, barf buckets and blood, the stench of unhealing wounds, the fearful cries of the dying. Up here, in transcendent splendor, with the city shining all around them, the Renowned Oncologist plied his trade. But for Queenie, this was a one-time-only visit. Everything was at stake.

"Well, I want to eat," Queenie said, a reasonable answer, hewing close to the essentials, her eyes as purely blue as the sky outside.

"That's the main thing. I'd like to hold down some food. Mashed potatoes. Cheerios. Anything."

The Oncologist nodded slowly. He understood. He had a golden tan. He likely spent his weekends on Nantucket or the Vineyard, maybe sailing over in his own boat, or flying in a small plane. He riffled through Queenie's file, examining the contents, seemingly bewildered, as if Queenie had just asked to jump out the window and hop a rocket ship to Mars.

"If we could eat, we'd have a fighting chance to beat this thing," said Husband.

"We?" echoed the oncologist, turning his gaze on Husband. The first person plural pronoun had stalled his gears. "What do you mean, we?"

"Oh, I mean she." Husband jerked his head toward Queenie, not once but three times, then blinked. "She'd be able to put back on some weight and have the strength to fight this thing."

This thing.

Renowned Oncologist fiddled with the fluorescent tab, Ruth Ann Malloy Quinn. The doctor took his time. He read and/or reread Queenie's documents with utmost care. No rush. At this level of the health care system— *health care system? Surely, an oxymoron!* — Queenie liked to joke — the docs had all the time in the world. No phones rang, no one else was waiting, no voices were overheard from other rooms. Nobody else clamoring for care. A stark contrast to the lower levels, i.e., the chemo treatment room with its awful noises and rush; the chemical and vomit smells; the awful clatter of rolling IV poles, the cries and lamentations of the ill; the soft soothing voices of the nurses, the lame and halt lined up outside the door, some weeping as they waited for their turn.

Regal now, Queenie watched him, her turbaned head held high, the veins in her neck and temples visible as streams, tributaries, through her fine pale skin. Her bony fingers grasped the armrests of the wheelchair. She was nearly helpless, this sweet Ruth Ann, just 47, a shadow of her former self, always kind and full of optimism, the good one of the six Malloy sisters with their matching heart shaped butts.

At last He spoke.

"There's nothing I can do to help you eat," he said. A shard of hope disintegrated. Big Sis, looking into Queenie's eyes, saw it disappear from the iris on the right.

He, capital 'h', might have been ready to say more, but Husband interrupted.

"But the test results." Husband jerked and twitched. He pointed to the folder in the doctor's hands. "Those test results say no tumor. No goddamned tumor, excuse my French. No Evidence of Disease. N.E.D. We're dancing with NED here." Husband stared at Doctor. He spoke as one great mechanic to another. "This is a whole new battery of tests, just done…No Evidence of Disease."

"I love dancing with Ned," burbled Queenie. "Doesn't everyone?"

Neither man heard. Husband stretched his jaw. Queenie tried to punch him before the head jerks started, but she missed. Big Sis was ready to do this for her, but Queenie read her mind, warned her off with a look.

"We're thinking it's got to be radiation enteritis," said Husband. "She had that radiation, the Intensity Modulated type, and it did her in."

"I'd rather die than go through that again," murmured Queenie.

"If it's radiation enteritis we can fix it, can't we?" Husband raised his hands in supplication, stared across the vast and shining desktop at the Great One. "If there's no sign of tumor, isn't it just a matter of finding the blockage and unblocking it?"

Big Sister's antennae began to quiver at the Husband's line of questioning. She felt him pushing the doctor someplace the doctor did not want to go. Queenie didn't either.

"It's not that simple," the Great One said, but Husband, who came from a long line of mechanics and was himself a whiz, kept right on going.

"We know a guy who'd do it, a general surgeon. I mean he promised us he would, if it would help keep her going for a little bit longer."

Keep her going a little bit longer.

The thing was, Husband could fix just about anything, especially complex and mysterious things such as motherboards, sound amplifiers, ride-on mowers. He was good with toasters, too. He set up Queenie's TPN with a little pump inside a rolling backpack so she could get around without attachment to an IV pole. Before Husband figured out this pumping system, she sat for hours while it drip, drip, dripped into her bloodstream from a hanging bag. With the rolling back pack, she could pee by herself, or hobble to the window to look out at her overgrown, untended garden. For Husband, everything came down to the mechanics, the wiring, gears, drives, widgets, sprockets, buttons, levers. Everything was fixable.

At last, the Great One answered.

"I wouldn't consider Mrs. Quinn here, Ruth Ann" — a nod in her direction, seeking permission for his intimacy — "a good candidate for surgery. I don't even need her file to make that judgment — I can tell by looking at her. She's just too fragile."

All three of them looked at Queenie in her shining silver chair, tiny Ruth Ann, fragile Ruth Ann, almost transparent in the high bright morning light. Big Sis put her hand on Queenie's. Her sister was in vibrate mode.

By this point, Queenie had survived half a dozen major surgeries, including a hysterectomy and, twice, the removal of lengths of bowel. Debulking, the cutting out of all visible tumor. Not to mention several rounds of chemo and 12 weeks of radiation. After a year with the colostomy bag her bowel had been reattached. That's when the oncs at Dartmouth Hitchcock had taken more than 100 biopsies.

"No evidence of disease," repeated Queenie.

Then, ever so slowly, it started again. Poor Queenie couldn't eat or poop. More tests and more biopsies. *Some atypical cells revealed. OK, some atypical cells, whatever the hell that meant, but no malignancy.*

"Her ability to heal has been compromised. That's obvious, isn't it?" He, capital 'h', spoke gently, understanding fully the weight and meaning of his words. "I couldn't in good conscience recommend surgery."

"But scar tissue and enteritis, they're not cancer, are they?" Husband voice was high-pitched, unfamiliar, a cry from the desert. He blinked and jerked his head. They waited for an answer the doctor did not give.

"Do you know of any studies?" Queenie asked at last, the old familiar Queenie coming out, the intelligent, well educated, self-possessed professional Queenie. She was coming back to herself. "Anything experimental I might take part in?" Queenie stared at the doctor. Hope and terror caromed in her eyes.

"You'd need to be much stronger than you are right now. You'd need to be stable in some way, and you're still losing weight."

A quick plunge to the bottom. Another shard went dark.

"All the tests say no tumors," Husband repeated. "You've got a new MRI right there." He pointed to the file. "Clean as a whistle. No tumors. That means something else is causing the blockage, and if we could only find out what it is…"

"Mr. and Mrs. Quinn," he said, oh so quietly, so patiently, then realized Big Sis was there. "And Miss? Mrs.?"

"Cho," she told him. "Celestine Malloy Cho."

"Mrs. Cho," he repeated.

"Ruth Ann's sister."

He nodded, then let the silence swell until it filled the room. An awful, blooming silence, a mushroom cloud. "The blockage may well be partly enteritis. And it's likely also partly scar tissue. But no doubt, no doubt at all, that it's also partly tumor."

Big Sis was scribbling on the pad when he said this, but would, forever afterward, swear the sunlight flickered; the world threatened to go dark.

"In my experience with this illness, there's no way it isn't partly tumor."

Technology can't always keep up with the disease.

"No dancing with NED?" asked Queenie.

"No dancing with NED," the oncologist repeated, but it was not a question.

In the quiet after this detonation, Husband cleared his throat and blinked. A mechanic, desperate, he rummaged through his box for the best tool. He threw out terms. Hyperthermic chemo perfusion? Bone marrow stem cell rescue? He had it somewhere, he was certain he did. Antiangiogenic agents? The oncologist kept nodding no, his palms together, and pressed against his lips, almost as in prayer. Big Sis saw him as an icon, carved in wood and stained, attached to the wall of a shadowy cathedral. Now Husband offered the names of medications, a litany, a lamentation. He'd spent hours on the Internet, in libraries, Husband had. He'd borrowed Queenie's PDR. He'd scoured all available sources for information; memorized a new vocabulary: Gemcitabine. Bevacizumab. Erlotinib. Pemetrexed. Ondansetran. Dexamethasone. Cisplatin. Carboplatin. Adriamycin. Words odd enough to bring on tachycardia. The poetry of cancer. The oncologist kept praying.

"With Google, everyone's an expert," he said when Husband finally fell silent. He turned to Queenie. "Mrs. Quinn, your timing is off." He shrugged beneath the weight of the great sorrow on his shoulders. He meant it, he really did. "I'm sorry to be so blunt. But some of these things your husband mentioned, we're not even trying yet. Others we're trying on…" He paused, inhaled and exhaled slowly, Zen breathing. "We're trying them on healthier women. That's the only way I can express it. You've been through too much already. I can't put you into a study at this time for the same reason you can't go into surgery. You're too weak. I couldn't risk it."

Everything was silent for a time until Queenie's voice, a fragile fiber, uncoiled from a great distance. "What should I do? What can I expect?"

"No new tumors means the Carbo-Taxol's working," the doctor said, opening her file. "It's keeping those tumors at bay." Paclitaxel and carboplatin, the chemo protocol prescribed by the oncs at Dartmouth-Hitchcock, the one most often used against high-grade ovarian malignancy.

"At bay?" cried Husband.

"That's a good result, a very good result," the doctor said. He did not look at Husband.

"You're saying we should be happy with her situation?" Husband's cheeks were flushed. He pointed to Queenie, who gazed out the window, some part of her already gone. Husband's finger trembled.

The doctor looked at Husband with compassion, or maybe pity, but still he moved his head from right to left.

"Maybe grateful," he said, "given the nature of this disease, and her original prognosis."

Queenie stared out the window, still in vibrate mode.

"Sooner or later, the Carbo-Taxol will stop working, won't it?" she asked. "The tumors will come back."

"There's no way to predict. You could wake up a month from now, and the cancer could go into remission. You've got to keep your hopes up."

"Hope?" Husband choked on the word. "What hope is there if she can't eat? If she can't maintain her strength?"

"You could insert a G-tube," the Great One said then. "A minor procedure. It will siphon off her digestive juices into a disposable bag. It should mitigate the vomiting."

"And if we can stop the vomiting," said Husband, "she might gain some weight?"

"It's worth trying," said the doctor. "It's a little thing that might improve your quality of life."

Queenie, hypnotized by the vast empty sky, didn't answer, another piece of her already gone.

"How long? How long do you think I have?"

Big Sis looked at Queenie. She'd wondered if her sister would get there, to that final question on her list. Howling. *How long?*

"A lot of that is up to you," the high priest answered. "With the TPN, and the G-tube, and the good result from Carbo-Taxol, you could live a long, long time."

Queenie turned to him. "What do you consider a long, long time?"

"I've learned not to ever make predictions." He offered a rueful smile, looking first at Husband, then Big Sis, and last at Queenie. "This disease is just too unpredictable. And we've got so little control. In spite of our very best efforts."

Then he got up and walked around the desk to shake Queenie's hand. He squeezed one of hers in both of his. And that was it. He was gone and with him went his shimmering aura, glowing at a distinctly lower wattage.

In a moment, Cancer Couple and Big Sis, too, were outta there, ushered by the resident, all the way to the elevator, then on their own down down down into the sweltering garage and the gritty world of terminal illness

"A G-tube…a f-f-f-fucking G-tube…I coulda figured that out myself!!" cried Husband once the doors slid shut. "What an asshole. And you're the one who had to see him. Happy now? We've wasted more time and gotten no help at all. What an asshole! Wasn't he, babe, an asshole? A big flamer!"

Queenie, slowly, nodded yes, but didn't speak, the two of them against the world, the way it had always been. Husband could not, would not, ever let her go. Big Sis held the handles of the wheelchair, gazing at the back of Queenie's turbaned head. The pad of paper with Queenie's questions was tucked into her summer purse, smoldering like dry ice. Howling. *I need you,* Queenie had said and Big Sis, her secret sharer, finally understood.

Queenie, aristocratic in her wheeled throne, surveyed her kingdom, the steel box of the elevator car. She couldn't ask. She couldn't tell. In a jolting whoosh, the car plummeted 20 stories. The doors slid open. The rank hot air of the garage, a rogue wave, rushed toward them.

Also by Julia MacDonnell

A Year of Favor

Mimi Malloy, At Last!

About the Author

Author photo by Morgan Triska

Julia MacDonnell, an award-winning journalist and novelist, is not now, nor she has ever been, a New York Times bestselling author. She writes much too slowly for that. Like Philip Roth's infamous doppelganger Nathan Zuckerman in The Ghostwriter, MacDonnell can spend days 'turning around' a single sentence; a week or more on a paragraph. So, instead of writing books she hopes will sell a million copies, she writes about the things that matter most to her, driven by the conviction that they might also matter to her readers. She often thinks of Kafka's declaration that stories should 'wake us up…affect us like a disaster…grieve us.' But MacDonnell has no wish to hurt her readers. Rather, with her quirky vision and lyrical prose, she wants them to be enlightened and entertained – and to, perhaps, have something to take with them when the story's over.

Fomite

More story collections from Fomite...

MaryEllen Beveridge — *After the Hunger*
MaryEllen Beveridge — *Permeable Boundaries*
Jay Boyer — *Flight*
L. M Brown — *Treading the Uneven Road*
L. M Brown — *Were We Awake*
Michael Cocchiarale — *Here Is Ware*
Michael Cocchiarale — *Still Time*
Neil Connelly — *In the Wake of Our Vows*
Catherine Zobal Dent — *Unfinished Stories of Girls*
Zdravka Evtimova —*Carts and Other Stories*
John Michael Flynn — *Off to the Next Wherever*
Derek Furr — *Semitones*
Derek Furr — *Suite for Three Voices*
Elizabeth Genovise — *Where There Are Two or More*
Andrei Guriuanu — *Body of Work*
Zeke Jarvis — *In A Family Way*
Arya Jenkins — *Blue Songs in an Open Key*
Jan English Leary — *Skating on the Vertical*
Marjorie Maddox — *What She Was Saying*
William Marquess — *Badtime Stories*
William Marquess — *Because Because Because Because Because*
William Marquess — *Boom-shacka-lacka*
William Marquess — *Things I Want You to Do*
Gary Miller — *Museum of the Americas*
Jennifer Anne Moses — *Visiting Hours*
Martin Ott — *Interrogations*
Christopher Peterson — *Amoebic Simulacra*
Christopher Peterson — *Scratch the Itchy Teeth*
Charles Phillips — *Dead South*
Jack Pulaski — *Love's Labours*
Charles Rafferty — *Saturday Night at Magellan's*

Fomite

Ron Savage — *What We Do For Love*
Fred Skolnik— *Americans and Other Stories*
Lynn Sloan — *This Far Is Not Far Enough*
L.E. Smith — *Views Cost Extra*
Caitlin Hamilton Summie — *To Lay To Rest Our Ghosts*
Susan Thomas — *Among Angelic Orders*
Tom Walker — *Signed Confessions*
Silas Dent Zobal — *The Inconvenience of the Wings*

Writing a review on Amazon, Good Reads, Shelfari, Library Thing or other social media sites for readers will help the progress of independent publishing. To submit a review, go to the book page on any of the sites and follow the links for reviews. Books from independent presses rely on reader-to-reader communications.

For more information or to order any of our books, visit:
http://www.fomitepress.com/our-books.html

Made in the USA
Columbia, SC
08 October 2021